THE CHINA CHAPTER

Dublin detectives link a murder to international crime

DAVID PEARSON

Paperback edition published by

The Book Folks

London, 2020

This book is a work of fiction. Names, characters, businesses, organizations, places and events are either the product of the author's imagination or are used fictitiously. Any resemblance to actual persons, living or dead, events or locales is entirely coincidental. The spelling is British English.

ISBN 978-1-913516-92-5

www.thebookfolks.com

To William and Sam,
for their detailed help with air freight operations

Chapter One

The fire engine turned out onto Annesley Bridge with its blue lights flashing and its sirens piercing the cool night air. It was only just over a kilometre to the address in Marino that they had been given by the neighbour who called it in, and the driver knew the area well. As they sped up through Fairview Strand and swung onto the Malahide Road, they could already see the smoke rising into the air.

"Well, it's not a false alarm, anyway, by the looks of things," the driver said.

"We'd better get another appliance out. It looks pretty bad," senior firefighter Jim O'Donnell said as their engine got closer. He used his radio to call back to the station and summon the second fire engine.

There were several people out on the footpath in front of the end-of-terrace house that was well ablaze. Flames were issuing from the upstairs windows, and smoke was billowing out from the roof space. Downstairs, the front door stood open, and flames could be seen inside.

The four firemen that were manning the fire engine jumped out and set about their well-practised routine. Hoses were quickly unrolled and attached to nearby hydrants in the footpath. Within seconds, two of the men had run up the path and were spraying water in through the front door, while another had put a ladder up against the house and was dousing the upstairs windows.

Jim stayed on the path and asked a woman standing nearby in her dressing gown, "Is there anyone inside, love?"

"God, I hope not. Tony Phelan lives there. But I don't know if he was at home tonight, he works shifts," the woman said, wringing her hands.

"OK, thanks."

Jim called out to one of the men at the front of the property.

"Barry," he shouted, "you need to get your BA on and go inside. There may be persons present."

The young firefighter came back to the fire engine and Jim helped him into his breathing apparatus, checking the oxygen quantity in the tank that was now attached to the man's back. Barry set his timer and went towards the front door, spraying water ahead of him to clear a passage into the little dwelling.

Inside the property, the front room on the right – the main reception room – was filled with smoke, but wasn't yet alight. Barry opened the door gingerly, hoping to avoid a flame over where the rest of the fire would feed on the newly released oxygen and cause a firestorm. He was in luck. The firemen's attempts to extinguish the blaze were working, and the fire was already subsiding, although smoke and steam reduced visibility to almost nothing.

There was no one in the room, so Barry continued down the narrow hallway towards the back of the house. The kitchen was hot and blackened where the fire had eaten away at anything combustible, but the flames had retreated under the constant flow of water from the men's hoses. Here and there, small fires were still flickering and Barry soon put them out. When he regained some visibility, he saw quite clearly the inert shape of a blackened body lying on the kitchen floor in the foetal position. The person was quite obviously deceased – Barry had seen enough dead bodies to realise that life had passed from this individual some time ago. With some sadness, Barry made sure that the inferno was not about to flare up again before checking that there was no one else in the property. He trudged upstairs, hitting his breathing apparatus off the narrow bannisters, and looked in all the rooms. He found no one else, so he went back down and retreated to the safety of the front garden.

Jim O'Donnell came up the path to meet him as he struggled to remove his smoke hood and oxygen supply.

"Well, what's the story, Barry?"

"There's a body inside on the kitchen floor, Jim. Definitely dead, I'm afraid. Probably a man by the looks of it, though it's hard to tell. The corpse is badly charred."

Jim put his hand on Barry's arm. "Sorry, lad," he said. None of the crew ever really got used to the death that was caused by fire in these situations. As Jim re-emerged onto the footpath, about to call in the tragedy, the woman he had spoken to approached.

"Can we go back in now, Mister? I'm bloody freezing," she said.

"I'll just get one of the lads to go in first to make sure there are no cracks in your walls, or no fire that might have spread through the attic. But I think it should be OK. We got it in time," Jim said, signalling to one of the other firemen and gesturing towards the woman's house.

"Any sign of Tony?" the woman asked.

Jim just turned away and climbed back into the fire engine. He had a lot to do.

* * *

Detective Inspector Aidan Burke was at home when the call came through at three-fifteen in the morning. He wasn't long in, and he was in a deep alcohol-induced sleep, so the phone rang several times before he realised what was happening and answered it sleepily.

He had left Store Street Garda station early enough, and dropped into Edmondstown Golf Club for a drink on his way home where he had met several of his friends who had just come in off the course. The group had worked up quite a thirst. There were eight of them in all, and of course they were buying rounds of drink, so Burke had to consume at least eight drinks before he could get away. In fact, he had had rather more than that, so much so that he needed to call a taxi to get back to his house, leaving his car at the club to be collected in the morning. Burke was no stranger to substantial quantities of alcohol, although he had been trying to cut back, as he realised it was affecting his work, and his life in general, quite badly. This evening was, therefore, somewhat of an exception.

"Inspector, it's Sergeant Miller here. There's been a fire at a house out at Marino – just at the start of the Malahide Road. The senior firefighter is requesting a Garda presence. Seems there's a body in the house."

Burke tried to focus on what the sergeant had said.

"So? Is foul play suspected?"

"They don't know, sir. That's why they want you to attend."

"Jesus! Right. But, listen, I don't have any transport here. You'd better send a car for me and get Moore out as well. No reason why I should be the only one to lose my beauty sleep!"

Sergeant Fiona Moore was Burke's number two – his 'bagman' as it were. On the surface of it, they had a lumpy sort of relationship.

Moore was from Portlaoise originally, although she had been living and working in Dublin for some years. She could be feisty enough at times, but her personality was gentler than Burke's. Although it might not seem like it to the casual observer, the two had a lot of respect for each other, and there was no doubt that either one of them would have put their life on the line for the other, if the occasion demanded it.

Burke crawled out of bed. "God, I feel like shit!" he said to himself, moving a bit unsteadily towards the bathroom, and in that moment, he promised himself that he would reduce his consumption of drink further. He brushed his teeth and ran a soapy cloth over his face. He decided he didn't have either the time or the inclination to shave, so he went back into the bedroom and got dressed. Then his phone rang again.

"Hi, Aidan, it's Fiona. I'm on my way to pick you up. Miller said you don't have a car. What happened to it? Was it nicked?" she said, smiling to herself at the prospect.

"Feck off, Moore. No, it bloody wasn't. I'll tell you when I see you. How far away are you?"

"About ten minutes, give or take. See you then."

"Great, I'll just have time for a cup of coffee," Burke said to himself.

Chapter Two

Having collected Burke from his home in Crumlin, it took Moore just over fifteen minutes to get to the site of the house fire. She pulled her car up well behind the fire appliances and other vehicles that were in attendance so as not to create a traffic jam.

The firemen were packing up, rolling away their hoses, and putting the rest of their gear away methodically. The two detectives got out and walked over to where Jim O'Donnell was overseeing the departure. The house was still putting out some wispy smoke and steam, but there were no longer any flames to be seen.

"Morning, Jim, what's the story here then?" Burke said. He knew Jim from other similar encounters.

"Morning, Aidan. It's a bit of an odd one really. There's a dead man inside – we presume it's the occupant, a Tony Phelan, but we haven't identified him properly or anything. And there's more. There's evidence of accelerant. The glass in the back door was smashed, and we think petrol was used to start the fire. Want to have a look?" O'Donnell said.

"No, I don't want to contaminate the scene any more than necessary. But couldn't the fire have broken the window?"

"No, I don't think so. If the fire did it, the glass would more than likely be on the outside. It isn't," O'Donnell said.

"Right. Well, I'd better get forensics out then. Are you guys finished up?"

"Yep. All done. I'll have the report written up later today. Do you want me to send you a copy?"

"Yes, please. Thanks. See ya."

Moore had been standing by, listening intently to the two men's conversation.

When O'Donnell went off to join his crew, she approached Burke.

"Shall I get the forensic squad, boss?" she said.

"Yes. The full monty. And could you get a few uniforms out too? I want the road closed till we see what the hell this is all about. And when you've done that, see if you can find out what's at the back of this terrace. O'Donnell said there may have been a break-in at the rear of the property."

* * *

Moore made the necessary arrangements and then went to see how best to reach the back of the house. There was a lane running down the side of Phelan's house, separating it from the next terrace of six similar houses, but it was full of smoke and debris from the fire, so she decided to go the long way round. She walked down the Malahide Road to Fairview and took the next turn to her right, which led her up behind the terrace of houses where Tony Phelan had lived. A short way along the road, where there were larger, red brick houses, the properties were replaced by iron railings, and then a set of large gates leading into a school. The school buildings were to the front of the extensive plot, and behind them there were playing fields.

Moore entered the school and walked around behind the buildings onto the playing fields. She could see the blackened shell of Phelan's house at the back of the sports ground and walked over to where the property had a boundary with the school, marked by a pebble-dashed concrete wall about five feet high. Moore didn't want to go in too close, in case there might be some trace evidence to be discovered in the grass, but she was able to determine that each of the terraced houses had a small garden at the back of their properties, running up to the school wall. It was hard to be sure in the darkness, but she thought she could see where the grass and weeds had been trampled down adjacent to the back of the man's house. She set off again, retracing her steps, to alert the forensic team to her discovery.

By the time she got back to where Burke was standing impatiently in front of the burnt-out dwelling, the forensic team had arrived. Blue and white crime scene tape had been put up all around the place, and white-suited technicians could be seen inside the house, bent over, examining the scene.

Moore brought Burke up to date on what she had found in the grounds of the school. Burke summoned the lead forensics officer and asked them to include the area behind the house and the lane to the side of it in their search for evidence.

"Look," he said to Moore, "I feel like shit. I've had very little sleep, and I need to go and collect my motor. Can you look after this for a while? You can call me if there's anything major, but I'd say they'll be faffing about for a while yet," he said, nodding to the interior of the house and the forensic team.

"Yeah, OK. Will you be in later?"

"'course. Thanks." He turned and went off to get a lift from one of the squad cars.

When Burke had left, Moore walked over to the 4x4 belonging to the forensic team. She rooted around and found a paper suit and overshoes, as well as a pair of blue vinyl gloves. Once suited up, she made her way gingerly into Tony Phelan's house, walking across the plates that had been put down to protect the crime scene.

Dr O'Higgins looked up from his painstaking work as Moore approached.

"What's the story, Doctor?"

"This poor fella has had a rough time, Fiona. He's been shot through the heart for starters, and as if that wasn't enough, he's been burnt as well."

"Christ – shot! Any idea what with?"

"I'll know more when we get the bullet out, but I'd say it was a handgun. Quite a small calibre – but I'm guessing now," the doctor said, standing up.

"Anything else?"

"Well, the fireman said that an accelerant had been used to start the fire, so we're taking swabs from underneath the back door, but it's petrol."

"Any sign of a receptacle?"

"No, but we haven't done the back garden yet. Oh, and I've sent someone round to the school in case there's anything there, but I doubt it."

"OK, thanks. How much longer will you be?"

"A good while. But I'll get the body removed soon now, then we can move around a bit more freely."

"OK, thanks, Doc. I'll catch you later."

Moore went back outside and noticed that the front door of the adjoining property was open, and there were lights on inside. She knocked on the open door, and said loudly, "Hello. Is there someone there?"

A moment later, a woman in her sixties appeared, shuffling down along the hallway in a ragged dressing gown that she clutched tightly around her. Her thinning grey hair was dishevelled, and there was no trace of makeup anywhere to be seen.

"Yes?" she said peering out into the gloom.

"Hello, I'm sorry to disturb you, Mrs…?"

"O'Brien, Elsie O'Brien. And you are?"

"Sorry, I'm Detective Sergeant Fiona Moore. I was wondering if I could have a word about the fire?"

"Fair enough. You'd better come in then," the woman said cheerlessly, and turned away to retreat back down the narrow corridor into the kitchen.

As Moore followed her, she observed that the décor in the house was very dated and worn, with peeling paint on the door frames and black traffic marks on the old floral-patterned wallpaper. When they reached the kitchen, she saw two other women much like Mrs O'Brien seated at the round table with mugs of tea and plates with the remains of homemade scones in front of them. Mrs O'Brien made no attempt to introduce the policewoman, so Moore did the honours herself. Sensing a little resentment about her presence in the tight little group, Moore approached the women cautiously.

"Did you all know Mr Phelan, ladies?"

Elsie O'Brien answered on behalf of the group.

"We did, surely. This is a good community here, Guard. We look after each other," she said to nods of approval from the others.

"Does he have any family that you're aware of?"

"He has a brother, but he's in America. Billy, I think his name is," Elsie said.

"You wouldn't happen to have a number for him, I suppose?" Moore said.

"Not at all, girl. But won't it be in amongst his things?" Elsie said.

"I'm afraid there's not much left of his stuff. It's all gone up in flames. What did he work at? Your neighbour, I mean."

"He works up at the airport. Something to do with the planes, I think," one of the other women piped up.

"And he had no relatives here in Dublin that you know of?"

"No," Elsie said emphatically, "and we would have known if he had."

Moore had little doubt.

"Have you seen any strangers around and about recently?"

"No, we haven't, have we, girls?" Elsie said, and they all shook their heads in unison.

"What started the fire anyway? I don't think he was a smoker," one of the other women said.

"We're still investigating it. We won't know till the forensic team have finished up."

This was met with a stony silence from the entire group.

"Right, well, I'd better get going. Thanks for your help. I'll see myself out."

Moore left the little house thinking that the legendary Dublin welcome was wearing a bit thin in that particular household, but, she supposed, they had all had a bad shock. As she emerged, she saw Dr O'Higgins getting ready to depart too.

"All done, Doc?" she said.

"Yes, Fiona. I'll be doing the PM at, say, two o'clock if you want to be there. The team are just finishing up in the back garden."

As he was saying that, a shout came from the back of Phelan's house.

"Over here. Weapon found. Stand clear." An anonymous female officer, clad from head to toe in a white suit, and with her head and face covered, was standing stock still looking down at the patchy grass.

Moore hurried back through the house and out into the back garden. There, a forensic officer was standing with a small handgun held at waist level with a pen through the trigger guard.

Moore took a plastic evidence bag out of her trouser pocket and held it open as the officer dropped it in.

"Thanks. I'd better get this back to the lab straight away."

Chapter Three

It was after five o'clock in the morning by the time Moore had finished up at the scene of the fire. She doubted she would get much sleep if she went back home. The events of the night would rattle around her head keeping her awake, so instead she went straight into Store Street Garda station where she was based.

After she had made a strong coffee in the little kitchenette that they had set up at the back of the open plan, she started to get things organised. She opened a murder book on her computer and put all the details that they knew so far into it. Then she linked up to the drivers' licence system to see if she could find Tony Phelan so that she would be able to download a photograph of the man, but it seemed that he didn't have a driving licence. She would have liked to access the Social Welfare system too, where there would be a record for the deceased, and probably a photograph, attached to his Public Service Card, but Social Welfare had not yet provided a gateway into their computer systems for the police, so she would have to wait till later in the day and put in a formal request.

Having drawn a blank, she decided to get a whiteboard set up. She wheeled it across to the back wall of the room and started to draw. She put Tony Phelan's name in a red circle at the centre of the board, and then drew lines reaching out from it in the classic spider diagram arrangement. She wrote 'Airport', 'Weapon', and 'Fire' at the end of three of the lines, and stood back to admire her handiwork.

"God, it's not much to go on," she said to herself.

* * *

Moore busied herself doing nothing constructive, trying to process the events of the night, until the clock moved slowly around to eight o'clock in the morning. Soon after the hour, her phone rang.

"Moore," she said.

"Hi, Fiona. It's Malcolm O'Higgins here. I just thought you'd like to know that we found a few more bits and pieces out at the house in Marino."

"Oh, good. Anything of interest?"

"Yes, well, the good news is that we found a kind of security pass for Phelan. You know, the kind that you wear around your neck. The bad news is that it's pretty badly scorched, but I can just about make out the name of the company that issued it. It's Jet59 – with the fifty-nine written in numbers. That's about all I can make out, I'm afraid."

Moore made a note on her jotter of the company name.

"Did you find anything else of interest, Doc?"

"We had a quick look at the gun. It's very strange. Most weapons like this we come across are nine millimetres, but this one is smaller, but not like the tiny ones you see in the movies that American women keep in their purses to shoot their husbands with."

Moore laughed.

"I must get one of those before I get married! So, what can you say about the weapon?"

"We need to do more work on it. I'll let you know later. Are you coming across for the PM?"

"I'm not sure. One of us will be there. Two o'clock you said?"

"Yep. That's it. See you later then."

When the call was finished, Moore turned again to her PC and started researching Jet59. On the company's website, there was a helpful brief history which explained where the somewhat odd name originated. In 1959, the first all-jet services from Ireland to the USA began with the introduction of the Boeing 707. But these were thirsty beasts, and the airport had to significantly enlarge its fuelling capacity to meet the new demand. A couple of shrewd businessmen spotted the opportunity and set up Jet59. As traffic grew in Dublin, their operation grew with it, and now they were the prime supplier of Jet-A1 aviation fuel to a number of airline clients. In addition to a good share of the Ryanair business, they boasted several long-haul carriers on their client list, including China Skies, Mondo and Fly Japan, all of which had regular long-haul flights out of Dublin with modern equipment like Boeing 777s and Airbus A330s.

Moore had an idea. She left a note for Burke, who hadn't appeared yet, and headed out of the station. She drove back out to Marino and parked a few doors away from the burnt-out shell of Tony Phelan's house. She got out of the car and waited on the footpath, looking back down the Malahide Road towards Fairview Park. She didn't have long to wait.

After a few minutes, a huge fuel tanker swung round by the traffic lights and started up towards her. Moore took out her warrant card and stepped into the road, holding it aloft so that the driver could see it. The man behind the wheel was distracted looking at the burnt-out house and kept coming. He only saw Moore at the last minute. Moore held her ground, and the truck came to a screeching halt, stopping just three metres in front of her. She walked to the side of the vehicle, and the driver rolled down his window.

"Jesus, woman! Are you trying to get yourself killed?"

A car horn sounded loudly from behind the fuel tanker.

"I need to speak to you. Pull over please," she instructed, a little shakily. She hadn't realised how close she had actually come to being run down.

The lorry hissed and wheezed as the driver moved it on to a bus stop bay a little further up the road and pulled up. The angry motorist who had nearly hit the back of the vehicle when it stopped abruptly made a rude sign and blew his horn again as he passed them both.

Moore opened the passenger's side door of the cab and climbed up into the seat.

"What's this all about. I have a full load on here, and I need to get to the airport or they'll dock my pay."

"OK. I won't keep you long. Which company are you hauling for?" Moore said.

"Jet59, of course. Why?"

"Do you know a man called Tony Phelan?"

"Tony, yes I do. Why?"

"Does he work with you?"

"Well, he works up at the depot. We often give him a lift if we see him at the side of the road just about here, actually. He doesn't have a car," the man said.

"What does he do up at the depot?"

"I dunno. I'm just the delivery guy. What happens after that doesn't concern me."

"But you must talk to him when you're giving him a lift, surely. What do you talk about?"

"Dog racing mostly. Tony loves the greyhounds. He goes to Shelbourne Park whenever he gets the chance. Anyway, why all the questions?"

"Just routine enquiries. Look, I'd better let you get on. Thanks." With that, Moore climbed down from the lorry back onto the footpath. She got into her car and headed back to the station.

* * *

"Hi," Moore said to Aidan Burke when she entered his office, "you made it then."

"What? Oh yeah, and I got my car back too. Sorry about that."

"Ah, you're grand. What happened to you anyway?"

"You know – the usual. I fell amongst thieves, as it were, at the golf club. Never again, I swear."

"Well, not till next time anyway! Did you get my note?"

"Yes. I'm just waiting for the phone company to get back to me with his phone records. We need to see if we can contact his brother in the States. Listen – can you do the PM? My stomach isn't up to it, and, anyway, I need to brief the Super."

"Yeah. OK. I'd better get over there – you know how O'Higgins doesn't like to be kept waiting."

"Right. See you later."

When Moore had left, Burke slipped on his jacket and went across to Nesbitt's pub just across the road from the station.

"Hi, Larry. Just get me a brandy and port, will you. My stomach is doing somersaults!"

Chapter Four

The charred, blackened body of Tony Phelan was already lying on the shiny aluminium gurney when Fiona Moore arrived at the mortuary. He had been placed on his back. Some of his face, which must have been against the floor during the fire, was still relatively unharmed. This gave him a very incongruous appearance.

Dr O'Higgins was there, dressed in his green waterproof apron, and wearing a blue cloth hat over his luxurious mop of hair. Two eager assistants – one male and one female – stood close to him, waiting for his instructions.

O'Higgins nodded to the female assistant, who approached the body with her colleague to remove the man's clothes. They started at his feet, gently taking off his shoes, and then cutting away his socks. They continued with the corpse's trousers, underpants and shirt, so that after a few minutes the man was naked. The young man covered his pelvic area with a muslin cloth to preserve whatever may have been left of Tony's dignity.

The body was a peculiar mixture of textures. Where it had been exposed to the fire, the skin was blackened and blistered. Elsewhere, his skin was almost normal, if a bit blotchy. In some other areas, extensive burning, with red blistering but no blackening was clearly evident.

O'Higgins made a number of observations into the microphone that was suspended over the table as he walked around. After a few minutes, he nodded to the two assistants, and they moved in again to turn the body over onto its front.

Tony's body looked to be in a similar condition from the back. The burning was less intense, but a blackened hole, about the size of a five-cent piece was evident, with yellow and purple bruising beginning to appear around the wound.

"That's what killed him, Sergeant. And we're in luck – the bullet is still inside. I suppose you'd like to have it?"

"Yes, please."

O'Higgins moved in closer to the cadaver with long, pointed forceps and expertly felt around for the bullet. After a moment, he withdrew the implement. A small copper item fell into a kidney-shaped dish being held at the ready by the girl, with a pronounced tinkle.

The girl took it to the nearest basin and carefully swabbed the bullet for any traces of DNA. The fragment was too small to hold a useful fingerprint. She was back a moment later. O'Higgins lifted the bullet and examined it closely under a hand-held magnifying glass. He used a small calliper to measure the dimensions of the item.

"Hmm… 7.62 calibre. I haven't seen one of these before. I'll have to research it."

"Did it come from the gun we found in the garden?" Moore asked.

"Probably. But give Simon here an hour or so, and we'll confirm it."

The young man spoke for the first time.

"I've done some research on the gun already, sir. I'm fairly certain it's a Norinco P762," Simon said.

"Fairly certain, Simon?"

"Well, actually, I am certain, sir."

"And where does one get a Norinco P762 from these days, do you think, Simon?"

"They are pretty widely available, it seems, but they are actually made in China, sir."

"OK. Well, let's get on," Dr O'Higgins said.

The post-mortem continued in the usual way with the removal of the major organs, which were weighed before being placed in jars of preservative. O'Higgins paid special attention to Tony Phelan's lungs. After examining them for a few minutes, he pronounced, "This man died from the gunshot wound, Sergeant. He was dead by the time the fire took hold. There's very little evidence of smoke in his lungs. It was either a very lucky shot, or a professional hit. Most people using a gun like that would probably have hit his arm, or missed completely."

"Can you get anything more from the gun?"

"Not sure. We'll need some more time. I'll let you know."

"Anything at all you can tell me, Doctor?"

"Not a lot. He's in pretty good shape, apart from the obvious. Mid-fifties, I'd say. Non-smoker. No signs of excessive alcohol either. Muscle tone OK for the age. I'd say he gets a good bit of exercise. A few old scars from wounds of one kind or another – nothing too serious though."

"What about the time of death?" Moore said.

"Impossible to tell, but not long before the fire broke out, I'd say."

"Did the killer leave any evidence – footprints, DNA, fingerprints or anything?"

"That's why he set fire to the place. Anything like that was destroyed in the blaze. Sorry."

"OK. Well, if that's all you've got, I'll be off then. Let me know about the gun as soon as you can, won't you."

"Sure," O'Higgins said, and returned to his grim work.

* * *

"How did the PM go?" Burke said when Moore retuned to the office.

"Fantastic… not! No surprises – except for the gun that killed him. It was a… hold on a second."

Moore pulled her notebook from her back pocket and flicked through the pages.

"A Norinco P762. It's a Chinese clone of something, and uses small calibre ammunition. The lab boys are going to do some more work on it to see if they can get some more information."

"No prints or anything then?"

"Nope. Not a sausage. Did you have any luck?"

"Yeah, I did actually. The phone company got back to me and there were a number of calls made from Phelan's house phone to a New York number – area code 212. So, I called it. Of course, I forgot they're five hours behind us, so I woke poor Billy up at 5:00 a.m. He wasn't best pleased. I've arranged to do a Skype with him later on when he's properly awake," Burke said.

"Oh, cool. Can I sit in?"

"Sure. Meantime, why don't we nip out to the airport and talk to Jet59," Burke said.

"Sounds good. Let's go."

Chapter Five

When they arrived at the airport, Burke pulled up in the set down area outside Terminal 1. Dublin Airport still hadn't cottoned on to the idea of charging people to set down or pick up passengers like they had in the UK, so you could loiter for a few minutes without causing a major incident.

"Nip in and see if you can find an Airport cop, will you? Ask him how we find the Jet59 depot. I'll wait here," Burke said.

"OK," Moore said. She got out of the car and disappeared into the terminal building. A few minutes later, she re-emerged and got back into Burke's car.

"It's easy enough. Drive on towards the exit road and take a left after the maintenance hangar. Follow the road around till you get to a pair of high chain-link gates. That's it."

Burke followed the directions and stopped outside the aforementioned entrance. A short man in a high-viz jacket and wearing a peak cap approached and walked to the driver's side window.

"Yes. Can I help you?" he said, leaning over so that he could converse with Burke.

Burke produced his warrant card.

"We need to see someone in charge. Can we go through to the offices, or something?" Burke said.

"Hold on. I'll ring through," the man said, walking back into a tiny wooden cabin.

"A man of few words, it seems," Moore said.

"Hmm. Or a jobsworth, maybe?"

The man came out of the hut and opened the gates sufficiently to allow Burke's car through. He pointed off to the left and waved them in without saying another word.

Burke drove in the general direction indicated and pulled up outside a low, drab concrete building with a Jet59 logo pinned above the only visible door. They got out of the car and went in.

The so-called reception area was grubby and small, but was manned by quite a cheerful young man wearing a T-shirt with the Jet59 logo on its front.

"Hi. How can I help?" the receptionist said.

Moore produced her warrant card and said, "We need to see whoever is in charge, please."

"Oh, right. That will be Mr Davern. He's in his office. Hang on a minute," the man said, squinting at Moore's card to read the name. He lifted the rather scruffy phone with a badly tangled cord and dialled a single digit number.

"Mr Davern. This is David at the front desk. There are two police officers here to see you. A Sergeant Moore and another officer."

After a few seconds, David hung up.

"He'll be down directly, officers."

"Thanks. Is Mr Davern a director?" Burke asked.

"I'm not sure, to be honest. But he runs the show here. That's all I know."

The outside door of the office opened again, and another man in a high-viz jacket came in, squeezing into the small space with the two detectives.

"There ya are, Davy boy. What's the story with that Mondo Boeing? Is it running late again?"

David tapped a few keys on the keyboard of his dusty PC on the desk.

"Yep. She'll be another hour and a half yet. She's just approaching the north coast of France."

"Great. Time for a brew then." The man turned awkwardly, glanced quizzically at the two visitors, and struggled out the inward opening door back onto the apron.

Davern appeared through the door behind where David was seated.

"Good morning, officers. How can I help?"

Davern was a tall, thin man, dressed in a navy suit, with his tie loose at the neck of a pale blue shirt. He was probably in his late forties and spoke with a well-educated accent.

"Is there somewhere we could have a word in private, Mr Davern?" Burke said.

"Oh, yes. Of course. Follow me."

Davern went back through the door from where he had appeared, and held it open for the detectives to follow. They walked down a long narrow corridor at the end of which was a partially glazed door. It opened into a bright, well-kept office that was in much better condition than the rest of the place.

Davern slipped in behind the clean, modern desk and invited Burke and Moore to take a seat in the comfortable office chairs in front of him.

"Now. What's this about?" Davern said.

"Mr Davern, you have a man by the name of Tony Phelan working for you, is that right?" Moore said.

"Yes, Tony. He's been here forever. Very reliable. What about him?"

"Was he due in work today?" Burke said.

"Hold on a moment." Davern consulted his own PC and moved the mouse around on a colourful mouse mat.

"No. He's just finished four shifts of night work, so he's not due in for three days. Why? What's he done?" Davern smiled.

"I'm afraid he's gone and got himself killed, Mr Davern. He was found very early this morning in the burnt-out shell of his house."

"Oh my God. Good Lord. Are you sure it's him? I mean, why? How?" Davern was visibly shaken by the news, and by the rather abrupt way it had been delivered.

"What exactly did Mr Phelan do here, Mr Davern?"

"He's a senior fueller," Davern said. He could see the slightly puzzled look on Burke's face, so he went on, "Sorry. He fills the bowser from the tanks here, drives out to the plane, and puts fuel into the wing. We don't have underground services here yet, though they are planning for it."

"Which airlines did Tony work on?" Moore asked.

"Oh, all sorts. We have contracts with several airlines, and we do ad-hoc fuelling too when something a bit unusual comes in, or something is diverted due to technical issues or weather."

"How many fuellers do you employ?" Moore asked.

"We have sixteen full-time, but in the summer, we take on a few extra to help with the increase in workload," Davern said.

"Is it a dangerous job?" Moore said.

"Like everything else. If you do it right, it's perfectly safe. Kerosene in its liquid form isn't very volatile. It's only when it's vaporized and mixed with air that it goes up. Of course, we have to be careful not to spill any on the floor. But all our guys are well trained and we use the best of equipment."

"I wonder if we could speak to some of Tony's colleagues, Mr Davern?"

"Of course. But they are all mostly on the same shift pattern, so his team won't be back on until the day after tomorrow."

"Maybe we could have their home address details, then?" Moore said.

"Oh, right. Give me a minute to pull up their files. Do you know what caused the fire that killed Tony? I presume it was at his house?" Davern said as he ran a search on his PC.

"It's an ongoing investigation, Mr Davern, but it may not just be a simple house fire. We are still investigating."

"Gosh. Are you saying Tony's house might have been deliberately set on fire?"

"As I said, we are investigating. We'll know more in a day or two. Have you got those addresses for me?" Burke said.

"Yes, sorry. I'll just print them out for you now."

A small black printer on a shelf behind Davern began to click and whirr, and a few pages of printed paper slowly emerged from inside it. When it had stopped making noise, Davern turned around and collected the pages.

"There you go," he said and handed over the paper.

"Thanks. That's about it for now, Mr Davern. Just one more thing. Do you have any CCTV that would show the planes being fuelled?" Moore asked.

Davern smiled. "It's a very big area, Sergeant, and sometimes the planes are parked way out on the apron. I'm afraid not. We have CCTV at the exit from the tank farm, but it doesn't cover the entire area. Sorry."

"OK. Well, we may need to come back and have a look at that at some stage, so please make sure the recordings for the last few shifts Tony put in are preserved, won't you?" Burke said.

"Yes, but surely you can't think this could have anything to do with his work?"

"We don't think anything, for now, Mr Davern. But he must have upset somebody pretty badly. We'll catch you later."

The two detectives got up and Davern escorted them back along the corridor and out into the reception area where David was chatting to a woman in her fifties who was holding a clipboard.

They got back into the car and drove past the surly security man at the gate and back into town.

Chapter Six

"Can you hook this thing up, Fiona. I'm useless with computers," Burke said.

"Yes, OK. Give it here."

It was nearly time for the Skype call with Billy Phelan in the USA, and Burke had persuaded one of the civilian workers to lend him their iPad to make the connection and set it up with an account for Aidan Burke. It already had Skype loaded on it.

Moore prodded at the screen and tapped a few of the icons before setting the iPad into a sort of cradle that allowed them both to see the screen easily, and to ensure that the camera captured their faces. A few moments later the iPad started making a sound like an old telephone, and Moore tapped another button on the screen to answer the call. After a little flickering and some jerky movements, the image settled down to reveal a man in his fifties, with almost no hair and a ruddy, thin face.

"Mr Phelan. Thanks for calling. Sorry about earlier. I completely forgot about the time difference," Burke said. He wasn't at ease using this method of communication.

"I have Detective Sergeant Moore with me here," Burke said, gesturing awkwardly to his colleague who smiled at the camera.

"Great. Now what can I do for you, Inspector?" Phelan said.

"Firstly, I'm very sorry for your loss," Burke said, but there was no response from Billy, so he went on, "I see from Tony's phone records that he called you quite regularly. Is that correct?"

"Yep. Most every week."

"May I ask what you talked about, Mr Phelan?" Burke said.

"Nothing much to be truthful. Just the usual stuff. Tony would tell me how he had got on at the dogs, and I'd tell him about the weather here and a bit about whatever was going on at work," Phelan said.

"May I ask what it is you work at?" Moore said.

"I work for the City. I'm in administration – you know, housing, services, water, garbage collection, all that stuff."

"How long have you lived in New York?" Burke asked.

"I came over in, let's see, must have been '86 – yeah, right after I finished school. There was nothing going on in Ireland. It was having one of your regular recessions, so I couldn't get work. It was easier to get a visa than to get a job at home. So here I am."

Billy Phelan had become more vocal now that he was talking about himself. Burke needed to get the conversation back to the deceased.

"Have you seen your brother recently, Mr Phelan?" Burke said.

"How do you mean?"

"Well, have you been over here or has Tony been to see you in New York?"

"No, I told you, we communicated by phone."

"And when you spoke to Tony, did he give you any indication that he might have been in trouble?"

"Trouble? What kinda trouble?"

"Oh, you know, money worries or anything like that."

"Nah, not a chance. I know he liked to bet a little on the dogs, but it was small beer, and in any case, he usually won, if he was telling me the truth."

"And he never said that anyone was bothering him, say, at work or anything?"

"Nope. Anyway, listen guys, I gotta get going here. Things to do, you know how it is. Have you found out what happened yet?"

"Our investigation is ongoing, Billy. We'll let you know if we find out anything."

"OK. Thanks. What about the funeral? I might make it over."

"That won't be for some time, I'm afraid. But we'll give you plenty of notice, don't worry."

"OK, guys. Say hello to Ireland for me. See ya."

The iPad screen flickered again a few times and then went blank.

"What do you make of that, then?" Moore said. She folded the iPad back into its cover.

"Not a lot. I don't think the answer to the puzzle lies in New York. Do you?"

"Not really. Pity. I could do with a trip to the Big Smoke. Do some shopping. Have you been before?" Moore said.

"What? To New York? Yes, I have. I got mugged coming out of a bar one night. Had my wallet stolen. But that was before Giuliani tidied up the place."

"Jesus – some cop you are!" Moore said, smirking.

"Feck off, Moore. Now what's next?"

"I'll get Dónal Lawler to start working his way through the list Davern gave us. He can go and interview them. I might go back out and have another chat with the neighbours. See if they have remembered anything. Fancy it?" Moore said.

"Nah. You're OK. I think I'll go and bring Heffernan up to date with all the information we haven't got. He'll be mad, but what can you do? Then I'll get off home. I'm knackered."

"OK. See you in the morning then."

* * *

Moore decided to go back to Phelan's house and see if she could get any more information from the neighbours. When she arrived out at Marino, she noticed that Tony Phelan's house had been boarded up. Plywood had been screwed over the gaping hole where the front door had been, and the downstairs window to the right of the door had received the same treatment. The upstairs windows were still open to the four winds, and the blackened frames and scorched outside pebble-dash stood as a reminder of the conflagration.

She knocked at Elsie O'Brien's door.

She could hear the shuffle of slippers on lino before the dark shape of the woman filled the glass panel, and the door opened a moment later.

"Oh. Hello, Detective. Sorry, come in," Elsie said standing back to allow Moore to go into the house. Moore walked on down the narrow hall to the kitchen where Elsie was preparing her evening meal.

"Would you like a cup of tea?" she said to Moore.

"No, I'm fine, thanks. Sorry to disturb you. I just wanted to see if you remember anything more about the fire."

Elsie sat down at the kitchen table and signalled to Moore to do the same.

"No, I haven't. God, it's a terrible thing that happened. That poor man. Do you think he died in agony, Sergeant?"

"Look, I shouldn't really tell you this, Elsie, but Tony was actually shot before the fire was set. He was dead before his body was burnt."

Elsie took a crumpled tissue from her pocket, and sniffled into it, tears rolling down her cheeks.

"So, I was wondering if you heard anything that could have been a gunshot before the fire broke out?"

"No, I didn't. I was in the front room watching the telly. Dear God. What's the world coming to? Who would have wanted him dead? Do you think it was a burglary gone wrong?" Elsie said.

"We don't think so. There wasn't any sign of anything being taken."

"But I don't understand. What's it all about, Sergeant?"

"Elsie, what sort of a man was Tony?"

"Just an ordinary bloke. He kept himself to himself, but he was a decent man. We'd see him at ten o'clock Mass every Sunday, if he wasn't working. And he helped Maureen sort out her drains a few months back. She lives two doors up on the other side. But he was quite a private person."

"Did you ever see any visitors coming and going from the house?"

"No, well… very rarely. The priest called occasionally, and there were a few casual callers – you know, them that collects for charity door to door. But that's about it."

"Is there anything else at all you can tell me about Mr Phelan, Elsie?"

The woman thought for a moment, keen to help, but even when she racked her brains, nothing came to her.

"No, I'm sorry, Sergeant. Did you talk to his brother? I think they were quite close. And, of course he used to go and visit him in New York a bit. I suppose he got cheap tickets, what with him working up at the airport."

"How often did he go to the USA?"

"Twice a year, or sometimes three. He used to get me to keep an eye on his house. Take in the post, that sort of thing."

"I see. Well, look, Elsie, you have been very helpful. I'm sorry to have disturbed you. I'll let you get on. Thanks."

Moore got up and made for the front door with Elsie O'Brien shuffling along behind her. At the door, Moore gave the woman her business card and told her if anything else came to mind, to call her at any time, day or night.

When Moore got back to her car, she sat in it and called Aidan Burke, but his phone went through to voicemail. She wanted to give him the information about Tony Phelan's visits to America that his brother hadn't bothered to share with them. When she couldn't reach Burke, she decided not to go home straight away.

Chapter Seven

Moore drove out to the airport to observe the aircraft fuelling operation and see if there was anything unusual going on. She felt sure that the untimely death of Tony Phelan was in some way connected to his work, but she had no idea how.

It was getting dark when she pulled her car up to the fence at the back of Dublin Airport. She had driven all the way round the perimeter and stopped near a set of gates that were being used by the construction company building the new 29-11 runway. Like most construction projects, this one was running late, so the builders worked on well into the night to try and catch up.

The gate was manned by a security guard in a high-viz jacket, who spent most of his time in the small portacabin adjacent to the entrance. But as Moore observed, he quite frequently disappeared from his sentry post for up to ten minutes at a time.

When she calculated that he was due another walk-about, she eased herself out of the car, making sure that the interior light didn't come on, and crouched down to crawl along the fence towards the open gates.

Just as predicted, after a few minutes the security man wandered off, and Moore easily slipped in through the entrance completely unchallenged and, she hoped, unnoticed.

Once inside the complex, she remained in the shadows and crept around to near where the fuel trucks came out onto the apron to supply the parked aircraft. She found a well-hidden and relatively comfy spot, sat down on an old plastic crate that she found nearby, and waited.

Most of the planes that landed were carrying passengers, and once they had cleared the runways, they taxied off to various boarding gates and disgorged their travellers. She noticed that the Ryanair ones turned around very quickly, and often set off again for a new destination with a different set of clients within half an hour of landing.

She was beginning to think her adventure was a waste of time when a huge aeroplane, painted in a distinctive red and yellow colour scheme, landed and came towards her. The noise of the two turbines was deafening, so Moore did her best to cover her ears, but still the din rattled through her entire body. The plane manoeuvred about this way and that before coming to rest out in the open, well away from the terminal, and shut down its engines. Moore noticed that it didn't appear to have any windows, and its status as a freighter was confirmed when she saw the name painted on its side – 'China Skies Freight'.

Almost as soon as the engines had wound down, a massive door in the left side of the plane began to open. It rose up into the night sky, until it towered above the rest of the fuselage, revealing shapes like igloos in the brightly lit interior. At the same time, some heavy lifting gear drove out from one of the hangars and stopped beside the cargo door. Steps were driven up to the side of the aircraft, and the regular front door opened. Three men, quite short in stature, immaculately turned out in black suits with clean white shirts and peaked uniform caps, and still wearing white cotton gloves, descended the stairs carrying small overnight bags and chattering away in a language Moore couldn't understand. The men got into a waiting minibus and were driven away.

Moore watched as pallet after pallet of cargo was extracted from inside the plane and taken across the apron to a large cargo shed, while new containers were brought out and loaded up. When this operation was apparently complete, all the handling equipment was taken away, and the huge cargo door in the side of the aircraft slowly lowered back into position. The plane now looked normal again. A few moments later, an armoured truck about the size of a UPS delivery van came out from the hangar and stopped beside the aircraft. Two men clad in full security gear, complete with hard helmets and visors covering their faces, alighted and went to the back of the van. One of the men stood guard, while the other opened the rear door and started taking out what looked like ammunition boxes. Each one was a shiny silver colour, about one and a half metres long and half a metre across. He carried these one at a time over to the plane. They were stowed in the hold underneath the main cargo deck, where passengers' bags are normally kept for a regular airline flight.

Moore counted six of these boxes in all. Each appeared to be quite light, and had hasps and padlocks all along one side. When these had been loaded, six similar boxes were removed from the aircraft and stashed in the van. The containers coming off the aeroplane appeared to be empty. Then the men got back onto their van and drove off. Moore noted the registration number of the vehicle. It was the only identification that she could see anywhere on its dark blue bodywork.

Next to attend the giant machine was the fuel truck. It lumbered out from the depot, labouring under its full load of Jet-A1, and drew up abreast of the left-hand wing tip. Two men got out. The taller man went to the back of the fuel truck and took down an aluminium step ladder which he carried to a point under the wing. Meanwhile, the other operator was attaching an earthing cable from the fuel lorry to the plane's body, to ensure that no static sparks could be generated and set the whole lot ablaze. Then the first man rolled out a large flexible hose with a special connector at its end, climbed the ladder, opened a hatch in the underside of the wing and attached the hose. In a clearly well-practised procedure, the second man started the fuel pump which would send tons of kerosene under high pressure into the plane's enormous tanks. The plane, an Airbus A300, had a capacity of over 50,000 litres of fuel, but it only took around forty minutes to complete the task, due to the pressure being used.

Moore stayed where she was, out of sight, while all this was going on. Once the fuelling was complete, and the fuel bowser had gone back to the depot, the plane was left more or less on its own.

Moore waited another fifteen minutes, but there was no further activity anywhere around the machine. She carefully left her hiding place and, still staying in the shadows, made her way along the wall until she was as close as possible to the Chinese aircraft. Then she knew she had to come out into the open to get across to the parked plane. She looked around for several minutes, and decided she would have to make a run for it. Crouching down, she sprinted across to the plane and pressed herself up against the hull to try and remain invisible. She edged along to the open hold door and leaned in to see the interior. She was surprised by the large size of the compartment. There, stacked neatly in two rows, were the cases she had seen being delivered by the security men earlier. In order to try and find a label, or some identifying marks on the cases, she was about to climb into the hold when she was grabbed from behind.

Her assailant was big and strong, and try as she might to wriggle free from him, she was helpless. She tried stamping down on his feet, but he was holding her off the ground, so that she had no purchase, and was unable to retaliate at all. Surprised by the ferocity of the resistance she was putting up, the man decided to end it, and delivered a sharp blow to the back of Moore's neck, rendering her unconscious.

* * *

Moore had no idea how long she had been out of it. It was still dark, though she could just about see the beginnings of the dawn over in the distance. She was at the bottom of a trench that was between two and three feet deep. The base of the trench was soil, and some puddles had formed, soaking her clothes here and there. As she looked up, turning her head painfully, she could see sections of chain-link fencing along the two edges of the trench.

She did a quick check of all of her limbs, and was relieved to find that they were all there, and seemed to be working, if a bit stiffly. It was just the pain in her head that was severe, and her neck was very sore. Moore struggled to get into a sitting position and then levered herself out of the trench by rolling her body over the upper edge. She was stone cold, and wondered if she was in shock.

Standing up shakily, she looked around. The China Skies plane had departed, and in the distance, she could make out baggage carts and fuel trucks moving about among the parked aircraft, getting them ready for the early morning departures.

She edged her way down along the fence till she got to the end where she was able to squeeze out between two sections which were not tightly fastened together. She then made her way towards the buildings, staggering a bit from the aftereffects of her ordeal.

When she got to the terminal, she managed to contact the Airport Police. Once they were satisfied that she was in fact a serving officer, they were very sympathetic, and helped her get cleaned up. They also took her across to the medical centre where she was checked over, and found to be in reasonably good condition with no lasting damage.

When all the fuss was over, Moore tried Burke's phone again from a landline inside the airport building.

"Burke."

Moore told the full story of how she had been overpowered and dumped in the trench while Burke listened intently, making appropriate responses as the story unfolded.

"It could have been worse – can you just imagine what could have become of me?"

"I see what you mean. Anyway, bring all the information in tomorrow morning and we'll see if we can get to the bottom of it. Now, go home and get some sleep."

"Fat chance!"

Burke was in fact very concerned about what had happened to his colleague. Despite his hard exterior, he was not without compassion. While he wasn't too happy about her going out alone without letting anyone know what she was up to, even though he had seen the 'missed call' from her earlier, he would have been distraught if she had come to harm.

Moore went home as instructed. She ate a light meal and had a shower to wash the remains of the grime out of her hair. She tried to sleep, but it was fitful, with her waking frequently as various horrid nightmares disturbed her. In one, she was in a cave with several wild dogs barking and snarling at her, ready to tear her apart. Later in the night, she was being chased down a long straight road by an aircraft that was going to catch her and shred her in its engines. By six o'clock in the morning she had had enough. She got up and made herself some tea and toast, and left for the Garda station soon afterwards.

* * *

Burke assembled his small team as soon as they had all arrived at just after nine o'clock.

"So, what have we got then. Dónal – you first."

"Right, boss. Well, after we got to Sergeant Moore out at the airport, we organised a thorough search of the area looking for her assailant. The Airport Police were keen to get involved, and they have a dog unit, but it was hopeless. It's just too big an area to cover easily, and for all the security they say they have, the place leaks like a sieve. There are literally hundreds of ways he could have got out. We gave it a good rattle, but after a couple of hours, we had to stand it down. I gave the Airport Police a talking to about their perimeter security too. With hindsight that could have been a mistake."

"Hmph. OK, well, you did your best, I suppose. Fiona, can you tell us anything at all about the man who attacked you?"

"Sorry, boss. No. I didn't get any kind of a look at him. All I can say is that he was quite tall, and very strong."

"And do you think he was hiding on board the Chinese plane, by any chance?"

"Possibly. I didn't see where he came from."

"What about the mysterious van that delivered the locked boxes?" Burke said.

"That's a bit better. I jotted down the registration number. It's registered to a company called Presswell Exacta. I'll find out about them as soon we're finished here. Oh, and there's something else," Moore said.

"Oh, what's that?" Burke said.

"When I was talking to Tony Phelan's neighbour – Elsie – she told me that Tony used to visit his brother in America quite often. But I think Billy told us that he hadn't seen Tony for years."

"Hmm, that's interesting. OK, well, let's get organised. Dónal, will you follow up with Phelan's colleagues. Talk to them all and see if they can throw any light on anything. Let me know if something significant arises. Fiona, will you get to work on that Presswell whatever crowd. See if you can find out what was in those lock-boxes that you saw going on board the plane, and who they were consigned to."

"Yes, OK, boss. I'll get on it."

Chapter Eight

Moore went to her PC and started the well-rehearsed trawl of websites to see what she could find out about Presswell Exacta. She began with the Companies Registration Office website and saw that the firm was still active and had been founded in 2002.

"Where on earth did they get the name," she said to herself as she scrolled down through the meagre information. The company had been registered with just one director, which was very unusual. The name was Cahir Flannery who was apparently fifty-two years old and Irish, but that's all the information there was about him. The registered office for Presswell was care of a firm of accountants on Wellington Quay in the city centre, Walker Hodge and Company, so Moore turned her attention to them.

Helpfully, Walker Hodge had a website complete with photographs of the two partners, Gerald Walker and Peter Hodge, and a long spiel about what the company could do for you in terms of tax planning, bookkeeping, preparation of accounts, compilation of business plans and all kinds of negotiations with everyone from banks to mergers and acquisitions.

Before contacting Walker Hodge, Moore decided to have a look on LinkedIn to see if there was any more information about Cahir Flannery, but, alas, there was no entry under that name that could be the man in question.

She called the accountants.

"This is Detective Sergeant Moore from Store Street Garda. I'd like to speak to Mr Walker or Mr Hodge, please."

"I'm afraid neither of them is here at the moment. May I take a message?" The receptionist was well-spoken and gave the impression that she had everything under control, and was probably a very good protector of the two men as far as casual enquiries were concerned.

"What time will either of them be there?" Moore said, not allowing herself to be put off so easily.

"I'm not sure, I'm afraid, but I could make an appointment for you for next week if you like. May I ask what it is in connection with?"

"To whom am I speaking?" Moore said, trying to keep the frustration out of her voice – but not trying very hard.

"Majella. I'm Mr Walker's PA."

"Well, Majella, I need to speak with Mr Walker today, so I'd be obliged if you could give me a contact number for him. It's urgent police business."

"I'm sorry, Sergeant, I'm not allowed to give out that information. Would next Monday at eleven o'clock suit you?"

"No, it bloody wouldn't!" Moore slammed down the phone.

"God, give me strength!" she said to no one in particular.

Moore was still smarting from her misadventure in the aircraft and was in no mood to be messed around. She put on her jacket and collected Dónal Lawler from the open plan.

"C'mon, Dónal, we have a house call to make."

Downstairs, she told the desk sergeant that they were taking a squad car, and when Dónal and herself were seated comfortably, she set off for Wellington Quay with the sirens blaring and the blue lights flashing. Moore parked right outside the office of Walker and Hodge and left the lights on the car blinking away. She hopped out and the two of them went to the dark green wooden door that had the usual brass plate alongside it. She rang the bell, and a moment later the voice of the girl she had been speaking with earlier answered.

"Police. Open up," Moore barked, and the buzzer sounded that gave them access to the premises.

The accountants' offices were on the first floor at the front of the building overlooking the River Liffey. They were well-appointed and nicely furnished, inasmuch as these old buildings with their wonky stairs and crooked window frames could be.

Just as Moore and Lawler entered the reception area, a tall, rather corpulent man in an ageing navy pinstripe suit emerged.

Moore ignored the rather startled girl and spoke to the man whom she recognised from his photograph on the company's website.

"Mr Walker? I'm Detective Sergeant Moore and this is my colleague Detective Lawler. We need a word in private."

While Walker was pondering his options, Moore instructed Lawler to speak to Majella and get her full details.

"Oh, right. Come in, won't you?" Walker said, gesturing towards his open office door.

The two went inside, Moore closed the door as Walker sat in behind a rather fine antique mahogany desk festooned with files and papers of all sorts. He quickly closed the file he had been working on to keep the contents away from Moore's beady eyes.

"Mr Walker, when I telephoned your office this morning, I was informed that you were out of the office for the week, and yet here you are, large as life. I would just like to say that it's not very clever to treat the Gardaí with that kind of contempt. It usually backfires. So, I'd like you to answer some questions for me without any obfuscation. Do we understand each other?"

"Yes, yes, of course. Sorry. Majella can be a tad over-protective at times."

Moore was still furious at having been messed about, but she continued as professionally as she could under the circumstances.

"Mr Walker, this office is listed as the registered office for a company called Presswell Exacta. We are pursuing enquiries concerning Presswell, and I need some information from you about it."

"You see, officer, we act as the registered office for many of our clients. It's handier for them to have a place in town if they have to meet the authorities. I can dig out the details for you, but it will take some time."

"Hmm. I see. Well, that's fine, Mr Walker," Moore said standing up. "I'll just pop outside and make a call to our forensic team. They'll be along in half an hour or so, and they are very good at finding things. Oh, and don't worry, they will have a search warrant, so it will be all nice and legal. See you later."

"Wait, wait, Sergeant. I think I might have been doing some work on that file last week. Why don't I see if Majella can put her hands on it?"

Moore sat back down and said nothing. Walker called Majella on the internal phone, and a few moments later she entered the room carrying a thick blue file with elastic closures at the corners.

"Thanks, Majella," Walker said.

"Now, what exactly is it that you want to know, Sergeant?"

"I'd like the location and phone number of their business premises to begin with, and then I'd like Mr Flannery's home address, phone number and anything else you can tell me about him. What does this Presswell Exacta do anyway?"

"Eh, they are listed here as electronic research, development and manufacturing. But I'm not sure exactly what they make, before you ask."

"How many employees do they have?"

"I'm not sure," Walker said.

"For crying out loud, Mr Walker. You do their accounts, don't you? So, you have the details of their PAYE returns for the year. Now please let's not start that again. How many employees? Are they profitable?"

"Twenty-four, plus Mr Flannery. And it's not a limited company, so they don't file detailed accounts. But, yes, they are doing OK."

"Right. Well, then, if you could just jot down those addresses for me, I'll leave you to it – for now."

Walker wrote the two addresses down on a piece of paper and handed it over.

Back in the reception area, Dónal Lawler had finished grilling Majella who was looking a bit flustered.

Moore and Lawler left the office, and when they were back in the car, having turned off the blue lights, Moore said, "How did it go with Miss Cool, Calm and Collected?"

"She wasn't by the time I'd told her we were working on a murder enquiry. She wanted to know if she was in danger. I reassured her – but only a little. I got lots of information about her though."

"I bet – like her telephone number, I suppose."

"Of course," Lawler said, smiling.

"You dirty dog, Dónal." They laughed together.

Chapter Nine

It took Moore and Lawler twenty minutes to get back to the station and swap their brightly-coloured squad car for Moore's unmarked Ford Focus. They set off again at once, this time towards Citywest – an industrial and office park close to the Naas Road. This was the address that Walker had given them for Presswell Exacta. Unit 54 in the Saggart Hill annexe to the main park, which was a sprawling arrangement of factories of various sizes, offices and even a hotel and a Spar shop.

They stopped at the signboard at the entrance to the complex and studied it carefully. They found the Saggart Hill section easily enough on the colourful map, but noted that the units only seemed to extend to number 52.

"Maybe they added a few after this map was created. It must be over beyond 52 somewhere," Moore said and moved off in the appropriate direction.

They got to the end of the Saggart Hill extension and discovered that the map had been accurate. The units finished at 52 – an austere grey metal-clad building with a sign declaring 'Falconer Windows and Doors' erected over the massive sliding gates which stood open.

They stopped the car and got out. They both walked around a bit, but could find no evidence of the unit they were looking for. Once again, Moore's patience was sorely tried. She walked into the yard at number 52 and stopped a fork-lift truck driver who was reversing rapidly out of the huge warehouse.

"We're looking for Unit 54," Moore said to the man who was removing his black ear defenders.

"You're out of luck, love. They stop at 52 here. We're the last one."

"Are you sure? We were told there was a 54," Moore said.

"Look, darling, do I look like a gobshite? I've been working here for eight years, and there ain't no 54. OK?"

Moore decided not to offer an opinion on his appearance. Instead she turned around and walked back to the car. She took out her phone and called Walker and Hodge. Majella answered the phone.

"Majella, it's Detective Sergeant Moore here. I need a word with Walker, and please don't piss me about. I'm not in the humour."

The phone went silent, and a moment later, Mr Walker answered the call.

"Sergeant. How can I help you?"

"Mr Walker, I'm out here at Citywest looking for Presswell at Unit 54, and there's no such place. What the blazes is going on?"

"Oh, sorry. That's my fault. All their paperwork is for Unit 54, but they're actually in 22A – that's at the rear of Unit 22, back down near the main industrial park."

"Jesus, Mr Walker. I hope this is accurate information. We'll deal with why you gave me a bum steer later." She hung up just as she could hear Mr Walker getting his excuses ready.

They found Unit 22 easily enough. It was a paper wholesaler looking much like all the other units in the estate. There was a lane leading around the back of the grey aluminium building, and Moore drove up the side towards the rear. When she turned the corner at the end of the warehouse, they were met by a strong steel gate which was closed and locked. There was no signage of any kind to be seen, and there was no one on duty at the gate either, nor was there an intercom visible.

Moore and Lawler got out of their car and went to the gate. They tried rattling it, and banging on it with the flat of their hands, but all to no avail. The place appeared to be hermetically sealed. After a few minutes, they abandoned their attempts and got back into the car.

"What now?" Lawler asked.

"Back to the station, I guess, unless you want to wait here all day till someone comes out. The boss will go apeshit!"

* * *

"There you are," Burke said a little impatiently, greeting Moore and Lawler as they came back into the station. "We need to have a briefing. Heffernan is on the war path."

Moore decided it might be best not to stop and get herself a coffee, although she was in desperate need of it. They assembled in a quiet corner of the open plan.

"Right. What have we got then?" Burke demanded.

Moore recounted the wild goose chase they had been on.

"Bloody hell. I'm surprised you let a little thing like a locked gate defeat you, Fiona."

"If we had broken in, anything we found would be inadmissible, so I thought it best to retreat and do it properly with a warrant or something," she said.

"And what exactly is our probable cause? No. You'll have to do better than that, Fiona. Now, I think you said you have a home address for this Cahir Flannery bloke?"

"Yes. He lives out in Dalkey." Moore flicked through her pocketbook. "Ardeevin Road, number 71."

"Very nice. When we've finished here, get on to the local boys out there and get them to check it out. No point running around on another jaunt unless we're sure he's at home," Burke said.

"Dónal. I want you to take a few guys from downstairs tomorrow morning and go back out to Phelan's house. Give it a really thorough going-over and let me know if you find anything of interest – anything at all. And while you're at it, talk to the neighbour again and see if she can remember roughly what dates Tony was visiting his brother in the States."

"Right, boss. What are we looking for?"

"If I knew that, I wouldn't have to ask, now, would I?"

"Sorry."

"I'm going to get back on to brother Billy and give him a rattle. This whole thing has driven me mad. For heaven's sake – let's do some detecting and find out what the bloody hell is going on!"

When the somewhat fractious meeting was over, Lawler went off to set up the following morning's examination of the crime scene. Moore loitered. She wanted a word with her boss.

"Is everything OK, Aidan?"

"Ah, ye know. The Super is up my arse about this thing, and that's only because he's getting it in the neck from the press and God knows who else. He wants me to expand the team, but I told him that if we did that it would take so long to bring someone up to speed that we'd probably have sorted it by the time they were any use. What do you think?"

"We're definitely a bit short-handed, boss. What about getting someone with a brain from Fraud to sit in? There appears to be some kind of commercial connection to this whole mess, and if we got someone bright, they might be able to move it along a bit for us."

"Hmm. I see what you mean. OK. I'll give Pascal Fleming a call and see if he can find anyone with a brain for us – though I might not put it quite like that!" Burke said, smiling.

Burke looked at his watch.

"Mr Billy should be up and about by now. I think I'll give him a call and ruin his day too."

* * *

"Mr Phelan, it's Inspector Burke from Dublin calling. Have you got a minute?"

"Hi, Inspector. Sure, what's on your mind?"

"Mr Phelan, the last time we spoke, you said that you hadn't seen Tony in years. Yet we have information that he has been going to the USA to visit you quite regularly over the past while. Could you just clarify that for me?"

"Now listen here, Burke. I told you – I ain't seen Tony in years. We spoke on the phone a good bit, but he hasn't been here. Are you calling me a liar?"

"I just want to try and clear up the apparent confusion over your brother's movements, Mr Phelan, that's all. Did Tony have any other relatives or friends in New York that you're aware of?"

"No, he didn't."

"I see. Well, how do you explain the information we have been given then?"

"I don't need to explain it. You're the damn detective – you figure it out. Now, if that's all?"

"For now, yes."

The line went dead.

Chapter Ten

"Sergeant, there's a Sergeant Wilkinson from the Fraud Squad here to see you," the desk sergeant said over the phone to Moore just as she was seated at her desk with a nice hot latte.

"Thanks, Danny. I'll be down right away."

Sergeant Wilkinson was a thin, young, fresh-faced man who stood at what must have been all of six foot three inches. He was dressed in blue jeans and a white Ralph Lauren button-down cotton shirt, with an expensive looking leather jacket. He had a narrow face, but a nice smile, and he greeted Moore with deference, even though they were of the same rank.

"Good morning, Sergeant Moore. Inspector Fleming asked me to come over. He said I might be able to lend a hand with a case you're working on."

"Hi. It's Fiona, by the way. Yes, thanks. If you'd like to come with me." She nodded to Danny on the desk who blipped the door so that she didn't have to use her pass.

"I'm Robert, by the way, but people call me Johnny. I play a bit of rugby," the new man said as they climbed the stairs.

"Fly-half, I presume?" Moore said.

"Naturally!"

Moore sensed they were going to get along.

When they got upstairs, Moore wheeled Wilkinson in to meet Burke who was in his office.

"Sir, this is Sergeant Wilkinson from Fraud. Rob, or is it Johnny, meet Inspector Aidan Burke."

"Welcome aboard, Johnny. Let's hope you can kick this one over the bar for us." Burke needed no explanation when he saw Wilkinson's stature.

Moore was surprised to find that Wilkinson had read his way into the case overnight. He was well up to speed and was already in a position to contribute.

"Presswell Exacta manufacture micro-chips. They are quite a secretive outfit. It looks like they have a few contracts with the Far Eastern phone and PC makers, and as you know there's paranoia about them at the moment. So, they try and stay below the radar. Their business is entirely for export, so if you want to get under their skin, try the IDA. They must have some info on them. I'm sure they have received grant aid of some kind."

"That's cool, Rob. Could you follow that up for us? We need to find out exactly what they are up to, and more specifically, what's in those sealed boxes they send to China."

"Yes. I heard about your little adventure out at the airport. A bit scary," Wilkinson said.

"You're not wrong. Bloody hell, don't remind me. I nearly ended up in Shanghai!"

"And no air miles either – tsk tsk," he said, smiling.

Wilkinson left the office and went to a spare desk in the open plan.

"By the way, I've been talking to Phelan's brother again. I'm not happy. He is adamant that Tony didn't visit him in the USA. But we have the evidence from the neighbour that contradicts that. Can you get onto Aer Lingus? I'd say Tony was an Aer Lingus kind of guy. See if they have any record of him travelling over to the USA in the last year," Burke said.

"Yes, OK."

"Nice catch, by the way!" Burke said.

Moore said nothing.

* * *

Halfway through the morning, Moore's phone rang. It was Dónal Lawler calling from the burnt-out shell of Tony Phelan's house out in Marino.

"Hi, Sarge. We've had a good root around out here now."

"Well, did you find anything?"

"Maybe. We found a bunch of keys on a keyring in his bedroom. It might have been hidden under the floorboards. It's hard to tell with all the fire damage. And there's an old notebook too. It's pretty badly singed, but forensics might be able to get something from it. It's all soggy and charred."

"Sounds good. Well done. Bring them all back here. Are you finished out there?"

"Just about. It's a terrible mess."

"I know. Listen, don't forget to talk to the neighbour about Phelan's travels. The boss thinks it may be important."

"I'm going in there now once I get this filthy paper suit off. I think she was out at Mass earlier."

"Ah, right. OK, well, see you in a while. Oh, by the way, we have a new member of the team on loan. Sergeant Rob Wilkinson from Fraud."

"Cool. OK, see ya later."

* * *

When Moore finally managed to penetrate all the annoying automated voice recognition responses from the Aer Lingus phone system – press one for this, two for that, and so on – and got to speak to a human, she was put through quite quickly to a manager in reservations. She gave Tony's details, in as far as she knew them, and he told her it would take a while to retrieve the records, assuming that he had in fact travelled with the airline. Moore gave the man her details and asked him to let her know as soon as he could.

While Moore was waiting for Aer Lingus to call her back, she had an idea. She knew that it was almost impossible to survive in the United States without a credit card, and she figured that Tony Phelan, being a conservative sort, would probably have his from one of the major banks.

She called the manager in her own branch to see how she could go about locating the details.

"Hi, Fiona. How can I help you this morning?"

"Hi, Trevor. I'm trying to locate credit card details for a man who lived in Marino and worked up at the airport. I'm sure he banked with one of the big Irish banks – either you lot or the other crowd. Any ideas how I could trace it?"

"That should be easy enough. Our airport branch has a deal with the employees up there. They don't pay any fees and they get a bit of discount on various charges, like foreign exchange and so on. If you give me his name, I'll put a call through and see what I can get for you."

"Gosh, thanks Trevor. That would be great. His name was Tony Phelan, and he lived in Marino, Dublin 3. He worked for Jet59, the fuel company out there."

"Fine. I'll let you know. Bye."

* * *

The first call Moore received back was from Aer Lingus.

"Hi, thanks for calling back," she said to the man.

"Hi, Sergeant. I found a few records here for your Mr Phelan. Let's see. Yes, he travelled three times in the last year to the USA. It was easy to find him – he went on standby as a staffer. We let the guys from Jet59 do that when we're not fully booked. It helps when we need a quick turnaround."

"Can you give me the dates he went to New York?" Moore said.

"Oh no, not New York. Tony Phelan travelled to LAX each time, sorry, Los Angeles. He didn't go to New York."

"I see. And you're sure it was LA?"

"Yes, certain. Round trip each time. Five days, four days and the last trip was six days, just last month."

"Listen, that's very helpful. Thanks a lot. Could I ask you to email me across the details, you know, dates and stuff? And did he travel alone from what you can see?"

"Yes, he did. A single booking each time. Just give me your email address then."

Moore did the necessary and finished the call.

She was about to go and find Burke when her phone rang again.

"Sergeant Moore."

"Hello, Fiona."

She recognised the bank manager's voice.

"Yes, hello Trevor. Did you find anything?"

"Yes, we did. Your man had a credit card all right. The manager at the airport branch found it almost at once. Would you like me to email across his statements?"

"Yes, could you. Thanks a million, Trevor. You're a star."

Chapter Eleven

Superintendent Jerome Heffernan's personal assistant called Burke on the internal phone.

"Inspector, Superintendent Heffernan would like to see you. Could you come up in about fifteen minutes, please?"

"Yes, of course, Maureen. I'll be up then."

Burke prepared for an ass-kicking. Heffernan disliked it intensely when the press was on his case, and there seemed to be no progress of any kind in a murder that appeared to have grabbed the attention of the public. So, the solution was obviously to lean on his team and give them a right old ticking off. That was bound to make things better.

Just as he was about to head upstairs, Rob Wilkinson put his head around the door.

"Got a sec, Inspector?"

"Just one, Rob. What's up?"

"The guys from Dalkey have been back on. They say there was no Flannery at the address we gave them on Ardeevin Road. There was a Flanagan up to about eighteen months ago, but he moved away, and they don't know where he's gone."

"OK, Rob, thanks. Make sure Sergeant Moore is informed, won't you?"

"Yes, of course, sir."

Burke climbed the stairs with a feeling of foreboding. When he arrived outside the superintendent's office, he asked Maureen, "How's the form, Maureen?"

"I just took in his coffee. He seems to be in good humour," Maureen said, a little nervously. She didn't really like talking about her boss in this way, but she respected Burke's rank.

"Right. Here goes," Burke said, and knocked on the superintendent's door.

"Come in, Aidan. Take a seat. Can I get you a coffee, or tea?"

"No thanks, boss. I'm fine."

"Look, I wanted to have a word with you about this Tony Phelan case. It's a bit tricky, to be honest. I've had a call from the USA. Quite honestly, I'm not sure quite who, or should I say, under what auspices the man was calling. Something to do with the State Department I think he said. Anyway, they're sending over someone they called an agent to talk to us."

"I see. Did they say what it was about, boss?"

"No, not specifically. They just asked me if I was in charge of the Phelan case, and said they wanted to talk to us about it. It's all rather cloak and dagger for my liking, but I think we should go along with it for a while in any case. We might learn something."

"Eh… OK. But I'd say they'll be wanting to get more out of us than they give us. What happens now?"

Heffernan opened his big hardbacked daybook and thumbed through the pages.

"He's called Guy Anderson. He'll be in on the Delta flight from LA tomorrow. Can you meet him and see what way the land lies?"

"Yeah, OK. What do I call him, I mean, is he Lieutenant, or Captain or whatever?"

"How the hell do I know? Just call him Guy. If he barks, you'll know you got it wrong. Try and keep him away from me, though. I've no idea how to deal with these fellas. OK?"

"Yes, all right. I'll keep you posted, of course, sir. Is that all?"

"Yes, that's all. But, Aidan, go carefully. I don't want this to get messy, OK?"

"I hear you, sir."

* * *

When Burke got back to his office, he called Moore in.

"How are things, Fiona?"

"So-so. I'm just going through Tony Phelan's credit card statements. It's a bit odd. He's been to the US – we already know that – and there are charges for taxis and other incidental expenses, but no hotel bills. So, either he has a friend or relative over there that he stays with, or someone else was picking up the tab."

"Hmm, well, that could be. Listen, we're having a visitor from the US tomorrow. Heffernan wants us to meet him off the Delta flight from LA in the morning. It's connected to the Phelan case, but I don't know how yet."

"I see. Is this bloke FBI or what?"

"Search me. All I was told is that the US State Department had been in touch, and Heffernan wants to keep his distance. Can you call and get me at about eight in the morning? The flight gets in at 9:20 and it could be early."

"Yes, sure. I'll track it on my phone and ring you if it's going to be in sooner. Delta from LA you said?"

"Yep. That's it. He's called Guy Anderson, by the way."

"Not very Starsky and Hutch. Let's hope he can shed some light on this thing. It's doing my head in."

* * *

Dónal Lawler arrived back at the station late in the afternoon. When he had got a coffee, he came across to where Moore was still pouring over Tony Phelan's credit card details.

"Hi, Dónal. You look whacked."

"Yeah, I feel it too. That house is an awful place. I can't help thinking of the poor old guy lying there frying. It's grim. And going through his stuff doesn't help. I gave the keys and the notebook to forensics. They'll get back to me. You got anything?"

Moore told Lawler about the impending visit from Anderson and the fact that she had recovered Phelan's credit card statements from the bank.

"Do you know if Rob has had any luck locating the boss man of Presswell?" Moore said.

"Dunno. I'll give him a call in a few minutes."

"Tell you what, if he hasn't made any progress, why don't you go out there early doors tomorrow? Be in position for eight when the workers are going in and make a nuisance of yourselves. We need to crack this open a bit," Moore said.

"OK. Will do. I'll leave you to it for now then. I'll let you know what we find."

Chapter Twelve

On the way to the airport, Burke was building a mental image of Guy Anderson.

"I bet this guy is way overweight, short, with greasy hair, and loud. He'll be totally preoccupied with his own importance and will think we're hick country cops. Wait till you see," he said.

"I'm saying nothing!" Moore said.

They arrived at the terminal and parked in the set down area. Moore spoke to the ever-vigilant Airport Police officer that was patrolling, explained who they were, and got her agreement to leave the car there while they collected their visitor.

Burke and Moore were leaning on the railings outside the Arrivals doors in Terminal 1. They could see the weary-looking travellers coming through, towing suitcases of all sizes behind them. They all looked tired and some were very confused, not knowing which way to turn. The more seasoned passengers walked away briskly, mobile phones to their ears.

The detectives could see Delta labels on some of the cases, so they reckoned Guy Anderson would be out shortly. They were just wondering if they had managed to miss him, when Moore was tapped on the shoulder from behind.

"Sergeant Moore?"

Moore turned to see a man about five foot ten inches tall with a good shock of black hair that came quite a long way down his forehead, but was brushed back to keep it out of his eyes. He had a longish face which was tanned, and dark brown eyes. He was dressed in beige chinos, a Lacoste polo shirt that was covered by a navy bum freezer zipped jacket. His shoes were brown Timberland loafers.

"Yes," she said, a little startled.

"Guy Anderson. Thanks for coming to meet me."

"Hi. We thought we might have missed you. Did you come through these doors?"

"No. I came around the back. You must be Inspector Burke," Anderson said, turning his attention to her colleague. The men shook hands.

Anderson had a firm, dry handshake. Burke thought to himself, *how wrong can you be?*

Burke took Anderson's suitcase, and the three went back outside, putting the bag into the boot under the beady eye of the Airport Police girl.

When they were seated in the car with Moore in the back, Burke asked, "Have you booked a hotel, Mr Anderson?"

"It's Guy. Call me Guy. Yes, I'm booked into The Arlington. I think it's quite near your station."

Moore noticed that far from being loud, Guy Anderson was quite soft-spoken. He was the kind of person that could melt into the crowd easily and become more or less invisible.

"OK. Do you want to catch up on some sleep?" Burke asked.

"No, I'm fine thanks, Inspector. I slept well on the flight."

"Oh, OK. It's Aidan, by the way. And my colleague in the back is Fiona. Shall we go straight to the station then?"

"Fine. I could murder a coffee though," Guy said.

"Sorry. That's very rude of us. Have you had breakfast?" Moore said from the back of the car.

"Kinda. Delta's idea of breakfast, anyway. But I'm OK. Just a coffee would be great."

Burke pulled the car into the car park attached to Store Street station.

"We can go across to Café Sol. They do a good range of coffees. Did you have a good flight?"

"Yeah, it was OK. Boring."

"Do you travel a lot?"

"Quite a bit. I've been to Ireland a few times now. It's one of the best places to visit," Anderson said.

The three of them spent half an hour getting their coffees in the café. All three were gently probing to establish some sort of relationship. They learned that Anderson didn't actually have a rank as such, but the two Irish detectives figured he must be quite senior within whatever structure he functioned.

When he felt the time was right, Burke said, "Right. Well, let's go across the road and get started."

The three marched back across to Store Street and Burke arranged a temporary visitor's pass for the American.

Up in Burke's office, Anderson started the conversation.

"Thanks again for meeting me. Can you tell me a bit about how Tony Phelan died?"

Burke outlined the circumstances of the man's death, and both he and Moore observed the perplexed look on Anderson's face as the tale concluded.

"What's up? You don't look happy," Moore said.

"Sorry. Yeah, it's just a bit odd. I can understand how he got shot – I'll tell you more about that in a minute – but the fire, that doesn't fit in."

"Why not, Guy? It's not uncommon to use fire to destroy evidence," Burke said.

"Yeah, I know. But apart from the gun, I bet you didn't find any other evidence of the killer. Or am I wrong?"

"No, you're right. We didn't. But tell us what you know about Phelan. Why is he of interest to you?" Moore said.

"Tony Phelan was working for us – well, sorta."

Burke looked at Moore.

"Sorry, Guy, I don't understand," Moore said.

Guy Anderson looked around as if to check that they weren't being overheard.

"Look. What I'm about to tell you is very sensitive. It's also classified, so it stays just between us, OK?"

"Well, I guess."

"This crowd, Presswell Exacta, are making micro-chips that are used in devices manufactured in China – things like phones, tablets, PCs. The American government is concerned about what exactly these chips could do – apart from making the phone or whatever work."

"What sort of thing are you taking about, Guy?" Moore said.

"We think the Presswell chips have some added circuitry that allows for information, such as the device's location, to be transmitted. It may include other stuff as well, like emails and text messages."

"But why would the Chinese want something like that?" Burke said.

"In the States, these Chinese phones are mostly bought by Asians. They're a lot cheaper than iPhones or Samsungs, so they go for them big time. The Chinese government likes to keep track of what their citizens are getting up to abroad. And it's an added bonus if a few US citizens fall into the net too."

"Wow, I see. I had no idea," Moore said.

"And Presswell is a very secretive outfit. We tried getting someone in there, but it didn't work. So, we then thought of someone at the airport. After a bit of scouting around, we came across Tony. No one in the wide world would ever suspect him of anything, so we recruited him."

"I see. And what exactly did Tony do for you?"

"He stole some of the chips as they were being loaded onto the plane. We kitted him up with a bunch of keys for the padlocks. It wasn't that hard. There are only about twenty different keys for that particular brand of padlock. When he was fuelling the plane, he dodged into the hold, opened one of the boxes, and lifted four or five of the chips from different parts of the consignment."

"Wouldn't the Chinese notice that there were some missing?" Moore asked.

"Yes, of course. So, we gave him some blanks to put back in their place. Then, when they got to China and tested them, they'd just assume they were duds – spoiled during manufacturing."

"And what did Tony do with the ones he had nicked?"

"He brought them over to us in LA. We paid for his hotel. We showed him how to pack the chips so the customs wouldn't find them. He got a little holiday and we got what we wanted. No biggie," Anderson said.

"Except that it got him killed. How do ya think that came about?"

"I guess the Chinese found out what he was up to. Maybe they put a camera in the hold of the plane or something."

"Do you think they sent someone over to carry out the hit?" Moore asked.

"I dunno. Not yet anyway. Possibly not. How many Chinese restaurants and phone shops do you have in the Dublin area – five hundred? More?"

"Probably about right," Burke said.

"Then there are all those students as well, not to mention acupuncturists and sex workers. I doubt if they are all upright members of society. Not to mention the hundreds – probably thousands – that are in your country illegally."

"I see what you mean. And if the killer was here, it would save all the hassle of false papers and arranging flights etcetera, not to mention the cost."

"Right. What clues are you following up?" Anderson said.

"Very few at present, but it's early days," Moore said.

"So, what exactly are you here for, Guy?" Burke said, keen to move on from the total lack of leads that they had so far in the murder enquiry.

"Ah, you know, just to see if we can help with any of this. We feel kind of responsible when one of our operatives, no matter how lowly, gets taken out. And while I'm here I can look up a few contacts. What, with the rendition flights through Shannon and so on, we have quite a few people embedded in Irish society. But right now, the overnight flight is beginning to get to me, so I think I'll mosey on over to the hotel and grab some zees."

"OK. Sounds like a plan. Want to meet up later?"

"No, thanks. You're all good. I'll stop by tomorrow if that's OK? Oh, and by the way, don't even think of having me followed. I can spot a tail a mile away in a fog!"

"Of course not. Thanks for your help. See you tomorrow."

Chapter Thirteen

"What do you make of that?" Moore said when Guy Anderson had left.

"I'm not sure. I wish I knew what rank the man was, or where he fits in. I don't like the thought of a loose cannon tramping around on our patch, however well intentioned. What do you think?"

"I can't help thinking he had at least one or perhaps more hidden agendas. Maybe he's here to recruit a replacement for Phelan. Or maybe there's a whole lot more going on that we just don't know about. Do we know anyone at his hotel?" Moore said.

"What? The Arlington? I don't think so, but ask around. Possibly some of the uniformed Gardaí may do. That's another thing. Why is he staying there? It's a bit downmarket, isn't it? I would have thought The Westbury or The Westin would be more his style."

"You're right. I hadn't thought of that. I'm glad you didn't mention the notebook we recovered from the house," Moore said.

Burke tapped the side of his nose with the tip of his forefinger.

"On the subject of which, can you get on to forensics and see if they managed to do anything with it?" Burke said.

"Yes, OK. And we also need to get to talk to Mr Flanagan. I'll see how Wilkinson is getting on tracing an address."

* * *

Moore found Robert Wilkinson at a spare desk in the open plan.

"Hi, Robert. Got anything good there?"

"Well, I have the famous notebook from Phelan's house. I'm just trying to make some sense of the jottings now. It looks like he had some kind of primitive code or shorthand going on. Shouldn't take me too long to crack it. And we found something else that may or may not be of interest."

"What's that?"

"There was a letter tucked into the back of the book from about two years ago. It was from McBrien Estates, saying that they had a client who was interested in buying a house just like Tony's on that road, and if he wanted to sell, could he give them a call."

"I see. I wonder why he kept it. Any sign he replied to it?"

"No, none," Wilkinson said.

"Did you get an address for Flanagan?"

"Yep! His phone number is ex-directory, but it's amazing what accidentally losing a few speeding tickets can do for you."

"I'll pretend I didn't hear that! Where does he live?" Moore said.

"Silchester Road, Glenageary. I looked it up on Google Earth. A fabulous old red brick number with granite steps up to the front door and electric gates. Detached, of course. Very posh."

"Great, well done. I'll see if the boss wants to come out there this evening when the elusive Mr Flanagan returns from Citywest."

"And there's something else, Fiona. I got onto the hotel where Phelan stayed in LA. They actually remember him. Apparently, he was quite a character, and the head receptionist is from the same part of Dublin. It seems Phelan had his rooms paid for by a company called Weltek Associates out of Chicago. I'm doing a bit of scratching around on them now to see what I can find."

"Cool. Let me know if you find anything."

* * *

Burke and Moore struggled with the evening rush hour traffic heading south out of the city. The Merrion Road was solid, so Burke cut up along Booterstown Avenue to see if the Stillorgan Road was any better. It wasn't.

They finally arrived at Flanagan's house at five to seven, and as luck would have it, the man himself was just going in through the gates in his sleek S-Class Mercedes. Burke drove in behind it and pulled up abreast of Flanagan's car on the gravel.

"Mr Flanagan? I'm Detective Inspector Aidan Burke from Store Street Garda station and this is my colleague, Detective Sergeant Moore. I wonder if we could have a few words?"

Flanagan was dressed in what is described these days as 'smart business casual'. He had a very well-tailored navy jacket that he wore over a pale Tommy Hilfiger polo shirt, with khaki chinos, and highly polished slip-on black shoes. His tall, slim shape and neatly-cut hair finished his elegant, if understated, appearance.

"I guess so. Would you like to come in?"

"Thanks. Yes, please."

Inside the house, the tasteful and well-kept theme continued. The house was double-fronted, and had a large sitting room with a feature bay window looking out over the front garden, while on the other side of the hall a spacious dining room, with a very fine rectangular mahogany dining table and eight carved dining chairs that looked as if they might be genuine Chippendale, gleamed in the half-light.

The detectives were ushered into the sitting room and invited to sit on the plain navy velvet sofa. Flanagan took up his place on a similarly upholstered armchair facing them.

"You're a difficult man to track down, Mr Flanagan," Burke said.

"In our business you can't be too careful, Inspector. But I'm not really that hard to find."

"What exactly is your business? We tried to gain access to your place out in Citywest, but couldn't find a way in."

"I'm pleased to hear it. All that money we've spent on security must be working."

"You were saying, Mr Flanagan – your business?" Moore prompted.

"We manufacture micro-chips mainly for export to the Far East," Flanagan said.

"Yes, and if I'm not mistaken, they are flown out from Dublin using China Skies. Is that right?" Burke said.

"You appear to know almost everything there is to know already, Inspector. May I ask why you have come here?" Flanagan said.

"Are you aware that there was a man killed who worked out at the airport recently? And that he had links to China Skies?"

"I saw something on the news about it, but I hadn't made the connection to the airline."

"Yes, he was working for the company that fuels those planes. But we have received information that he may have been helping himself to some of your micro-chips," Moore said.

"That's impossible. The product is taken in secure transport directly from the factory to the aircraft in sealed aluminium containers. We would know if any were missing. The customer would tell us as soon as they received the consignment."

"It appears that the man may have had a set of keys to the containers, Mr Flanagan. Has your customer reported anything odd about recent shipments?"

"No, nothing. All shipments have been complete and within tolerance for defects. We get a report on each shipment. I don't understand how they wouldn't have noticed if there were products missing."

"Apparently, some duff stock was substituted for the real thing, and the boxes locked up again."

"But this is ridiculous. What would an aircraft fueller do with a few of our chips? It doesn't make sense."

Moore glanced at her boss and shook her head imperceptibly from side to side.

"We're still looking into that, Mr Flanagan. May I ask if you have to have a licence to manufacture those things?"

Flanagan gave a little ironic laugh.

"Tell me about it. We have to be licensed by five different international authorities, and the software that runs on them is also subject to licence, so that's another whole rake of paperwork and nonsense. It consumes more than twenty percent of our production costs."

"If you don't mind me asking, I thought the Chinese were experts in this field. Why can't they make their own circuits?" Moore asked.

"Yes, and we have to be careful that they don't rip us off, so we keep upgrading the functionality. We don't mind if they copy last year's and put them into really cheap devices. We're targeting the top-end stuff, and that protects us a bit."

"What sort of functionality are you working on just now?" Moore said.

"I'm sorry, Sergeant, if I told you that, I'd have to kill you," Flanagan said.

Moore stared coldly at the man.

"Oops. Sorry!"

Burke picked up the thread.

"So, you're saying you knew nothing of this pilfering, is that right?"

"Nothing at all, Inspector. But of course, I'm concerned. Have you any idea where these stolen chips ended up?"

"As I said, Mr Flanagan, we're working on it. But maybe you can tell us who might be interested in them."

Flanagan snorted.

"Any of our competitors, obviously. But I can't see them killing for it. Maybe some foreign power – the Russians, or maybe the Indians."

"Do you manufacture solely for the Chinese market?" Moore said.

"Yes, we do now. We used to make for the Koreans too, but now it's exclusively China. They insisted, and it's very much worth our while financially. I guess we'll have to overhaul our security measures, though I thought we had it sussed. More bloody expense."

Burke got up from the very comfortable sofa, and Moore followed his lead.

"Righto, Mr Flanagan, we'll leave it at that for now. We may need to speak to you again as more information emerges. In the meantime, if anything at all occurs to you, please give me a call," Burke said, giving Flanagan his card.

"Yes, of course."

Chapter Fourteen

When Moore got to work the following morning, Robert Wilkinson was already at his desk.

"Hi, Fiona. Have you got a minute?"

"Yes, sure. Fancy a coffee?"

"Thanks, yes please. Milk, no sugar."

Moore went off to the makeshift kitchenette at the back of the office and made two coffees. She gave one to Wilkinson and sat down beside him.

"Thanks. I was doing some more digging on your Mr Phelan yesterday. A few things came up."

"Great. What have you got?"

"Well, he had a bank account here with Citicorp down in the IFSC. It was a dollar account, and I'm getting the records sent over now. There's a balance of $7500 in it at the moment, and it's pretty active," Wilkinson said.

"Wow. Let me know when you get the details and we'll have a look at them. Anything else?"

"I'm still trying to decipher his notebook. It looks as if it may be a series of dates and perhaps quantities. It's not very meaningful. I'm going to cross reference it with his trips to LA and see if I can extract more information."

Just then, the phone on Wilkinson's desk rang.

"This is the front desk. Is Sergeant Moore about at all? I can't get her on her own phone."

"Yes, she's here with me. Hold on."

Wilkinson handed Moore the phone.

"Hello, Sergeant. We've had a call from The Arlington Hotel across the river. They're a bit concerned about one of their guests. He didn't come back last night, and his bed hasn't been slept in, but his wallet and passport are on the dressing table."

"OK. But that's hardly a police matter, is it?"

"The manager says he's concerned. The guest had a meal in his room at around 9:00 p.m. and it looked for all the world as if he was in for the night. And the night porter didn't see him go out."

"OK, OK. I'll ask Dónal Lawler to drop over later, though he'll probably have turned up by then. What is the guest's name?"

"Anderson. Guy Anderson. He's an American."

"Oh shit! Thanks, Danny, I'll take it from here."

* * *

The Arlington Hotel was on the river, close to O'Connell Bridge. It had rooms both facing out onto the quays, and at the back overlooking a narrow lane. Anderson's room was at the rear, which was quieter, but didn't have the same interesting view of the city.

The room was on the second floor, close to the stairs. It was relatively spacious, with two single beds, and quite a lot of brown furniture. The manager of the hotel had accompanied the two detectives upstairs and opened Anderson's room with his pass key.

"What made you call us?" Moore asked.

"Mr Anderson had ordered breakfast in his room for eight o'clock, and when the porter brought it up, there was no reply. At first, he thought the man might have been ill, so he came and fetched me, and I opened the room with the pass key and found it empty."

"What time did he order breakfast?" Lawler said.

"Last night, just after nine."

"Did anyone see him after that?" Moore said.

"No, we didn't. I asked the receptionist that was on last night, and the night porter, and no one saw him go out," the manager said.

Moore went over to the window and drew back the curtains. The window was a simple sash type, with two separate panes of glass dissecting the window frame horizontally. It had a hasp where the two halves met that could be swivelled to secure the arrangement, but it was not engaged. She lifted the lower frame which slid up easily and leaned out. She noticed that there was a metal fire escape attached to the back of the building that could be reached easily from the window by someone reasonably fit.

While Moore was investigating the window, Lawler had donned blue vinyl gloves and was going through the American's effects on the dressing table. There was some loose change, a comb and a crumpled white handkerchief on the dresser. Lawler opened the only drawer in the piece of furniture. Inside there was an American passport which belonged to Guy Anderson, and several identical business cards with his name, describing him as a 'Senior consultant' for Weltek Associates. Lawler noticed that there was no address or phone number on the business cards, just a website.

Lawler took out his phone and took a photograph of Anderson's passport.

"Anything there?" Moore said when she had closed the window again.

Lawler handed her the business cards.

"I've seen that name – Weltek – somewhere before. Bring those with us." She then turned to the hotel manager.

"I'm going to have to ask you to keep this room sealed off. We need to get our fingerprints guys over to examine the room properly. And before we go, I need to look under the mattress. I hope you don't mind."

"No, that's fine. But if I may ask, why do you need to fingerprint the room?"

Moore nodded to Lawler who lifted the mattress on each bed in turn while Moore looked underneath. There was nothing.

"Well, it looks like either Mr Anderson went out through the window and down the fire escape, or perhaps someone came in that way and took him, if what you say is correct that no one saw him go out through the lobby."

"Crikey! Who is this guy anyway? What's all this about, officer?" the manager said.

"Don't worry, sir. It's not as crazy as it looks. Mr Anderson is known to us. We need to find out what happened to him, that's all. Please do let us know if he comes back, won't you?"

"Yes, yes of course."

Moore and Lawler left the hotel and walked back down the quays to O'Connell Street, across onto Eden Quay, along Beresford Place and around the back of Gardiner Street to cut down by Isaac's Hostel to the station. On the way, Lawler said to Moore, "What do you make of all that, Sarge?"

"It's bloody odd. I knew that guy was up to something. Trouble is, if he's been got at by someone over here, it will bring down a shitstorm on us. I'd better tell Burke as soon as we get back. He'll need to brief the Super."

"Do you think he was taken?"

"No, not really. There's no sign of a struggle in the room. But I'd love to know why he went out over the fire escape and not down through the lobby. Maybe he thought we were following him, or perhaps someone else. Anyway, we need to find him before the USA decide to invade us!"

* * *

Burke was not at all happy with the news Moore and Lawler brought to him at the station.

"Jesus, that's all we need! Are you sure he hasn't just gone out for a walk around the city? His body clock will be all over the place after the flight what with the time difference."

"I don't think so, boss. He'd hardly have gone before breakfast, would he? And remember the bed hadn't been slept in, so it was a night-time adventure by the look of it," Moore said.

An anxious silence filled the small office while Burke contemplated the situation.

"OK. Well, this is what we'll do. I better go upstairs and tell the Super. Christ! He'll be livid. But he may need to inform the American authorities, or whoever informed him of Anderson's arrival. When I've done that, let's split into two teams. I'll work with Dónal here on the missing American. You keep going with Wilkinson on the Phelan case. And let me know if you need more resources, this could get very messy."

Chapter Fifteen

When Guy Anderson left the Garda station and arrived back at his hotel, he did have a nap. But he was well used to working at odd hours, so by early evening he was quite refreshed and ready to get working again.

He started by making several long-distance phone calls back to the States where he spoke to a number of his colleagues and contacts. Armed with several names and numbers, he then started calling around Dublin, and on the fourth attempt, he hit his mark.

"Hi there. Is that Joe, Joe Donnelly?" he said when the phone was answered.

"Yeah, that's me. Who is calling?"

"My name is Guy Anderson. I'm a friend of your workmate Tony Phelan. I'm very sorry to hear about his death. Terrible business."

Joe Donnelly went quiet. He recognised the caller's accent, but wasn't sure why an American would be friendly with Tony, although he was aware that Phelan had been to the USA a few times.

When Donnelly made no reply, Anderson went on, "I was wondering if we could meet up maybe? I'd like to talk to you about Tony."

"I suppose. But I'm working today. My shift doesn't finish till nine tonight. What is it you want anyway?"

"I'd prefer to keep that till we meet, Joe. So, can we say ten o'clock tonight? Where's handy for you?"

"There's an old pub round the back of the airport. It's called The Boot Inn. It won't be busy at that time of night. We can meet there. How will I know you?" Donnelly said.

"Don't worry about that. I'll be able to spot you easily enough. Till ten o'clock then. Thanks, Joe."

When the call was over, Anderson rummaged in his bag and took out the printer. He hooked the little Sprocket up to his phone and printed off a photo of Joe Donnelly that he had been sent, and put the picture into his shirt pocket. Then he took the SIM card out of the phone he had used to call Donnelly and cut it into pieces, flushing it down the toilet in his bathroom. He opened a new SIM, put it in the phone, and activated it. He would go out and buy some credit in one of the local shops a bit later.

* * *

When the call with the American was over, Joe Donnelly got to thinking. The team that worked for Jet59 were tight, and each and every one of them had been deeply shocked by what had happened to their colleague. They had worked together for years and had formed a very close bond over that time.

When Donnelly had thought about the situation for an hour or two, an opportunity to tell the rest of the men about the phone call arose. The team had a break at seven o'clock for half an hour. It was an odd time for it, but it was convenient, as it was in between demands for their services fuelling Ryanair's Boeing 737s.

They gathered around in the small portacabin that was used for tea breaks and lunch. Each man had brought a snack, and they boiled a kettle for tea. When they were seated, Joe told them about the phone call he had taken from the American. When he had finished outlining the plan to meet Anderson after the shift, one of the others spoke up.

"Do you think this turkey had anything to do with Tony's death?"

"Looks like it to me. You can't trust those bloody Yanks. Just look at what their politicians get up to. Bloody blaggards, the lot of them," Donnelly said.

The men ruminated on what Joe had said. When they had all had a chance to digest the situation, Joe said, "Are you with me then?"

"Aye, we are. Someone has to pay for what they did to Tony."

* * *

Anderson wanted no one to know of his rendezvous with Joe Donnelly. He was still quite certain that the Irish police were somehow tracking his movements – that's what he would do if the situation was reversed, after all. So, he left his room at just after nine o'clock using the fire escape at the rear of the hotel, and found the GoCar parked at the end of the laneway where he had spotted it earlier. He had signed up for GoCar – an arrangement that allows you take a car from any one of several handy locations in the city and drive it for an hour or two on a pay-per-use basis.

He hooked his phone up to the car's Bluetooth and used Google Maps to locate The Boot Inn. The system advised that it would take him thirty-five minutes to get to his destination, and it started issuing instructions in a softly-spoken female voice, describing the roundabouts en route as 'traffic circles'.

He arrived at the pub as predicted at shortly before ten, and parked at the side of the road a little way back from the entrance. There were only one or two other cars around, confirming Joe's assertion that the place would be quiet. He got out of the car and walked towards the door. As he passed a narrow, poorly lit opening at the side of the building, three men jumped out and grabbed him. He struggled, but as he was taken totally unawares, he soon succumbed to the men, who were strong and fit. In less than two minutes he was bound hand and foot, gagged with duct tape, and had a dirty canvas bag over his head.

The men bundled Anderson into the boot of a car, which then drove off along the back roads surrounding the airport. They turned down a narrow track, and in through a gate that they had left open earlier, close to the fuel depot.

"What are we going to do with him now?" one of the men asked.

We'll put him in the old shipping container for now. And then tomorrow night, we'll load him into the back of the Chinese A300 and let them deal with him when it gets to Shanghai."

"What about water and food?" the third man said.

"I'll make a hole in the tape and leave him a bottle of water. He looks well fed enough to fast for a day or two. It's what he deserves, anyway."

The airport had quietened down quite a bit by the time they got back to the fuel dump. Apart from themselves, there were very few people about, and they were able to transfer Anderson from the boot of the old Nissan to the dark green shipping container unseen. He kicked and grunted a lot during the transfer, but the men had trussed him up well, and there was nothing he could do about his plight.

Inside the container, Joe Donnelly made a hole in the duct tape gag and left a plastic bottle of water in the captive's hands.

"Don't spill that. It's all you're getting, so make the most of it," Donnelly said.

Then Joe searched the man's pockets and removed his mobile phone. He undid Anderson's shoes, removed them, and took the belt from his trousers away too.

When the door of the container closed with a resounding thud, Anderson started to contemplate his fate.

"Shit! I should have told the cops what I was up to. I'm in real trouble now," he said to himself.

Chapter Sixteen

When Burke had gone upstairs to inform Superintendent Jerome Heffernan of the latest developments, Fiona Moore found Robert Wilkinson to bring him up to date.

"Blimey. What do you think has happened to him?" Wilkinson said.

"Nothing good, that's for sure. But he's not our concern for the moment. The boss is looking after that with Dónal. We are to pursue enquiries about Tony Phelan's murder."

"I'm sorry, Fiona, but I'm a bit out of my depth here. I'm used to following up frauds of one kind or another – chasing down cash transfers, dodgy money laundering and the like. I've very little experience with murder," Wilkinson said.

"Don't worry, just follow my lead. You'll be fine," Moore said, but she wasn't sure.

"What's your plan, then?"

"Can you give Mr Davern from Jet59 a call. I'd like to know when the crew that Tony Phelan worked with have their next shift. I think we could learn something from talking to them again."

"OK. Will do."

Wilkinson was back a few minutes later.

"They're all on a 12-to-9 shift today, so they should be clocking on soon."

"Excellent. Let's get out there and have a wee chat then."

* * *

The late morning traffic up through Dorset Street and on into Glasnevin and Drumcondra was slow, as usual, and it took the detectives over half an hour to reach the airport. As they completed the final part of the journey after Santry, a Ryanair Boeing 737 skimmed by overhead, its wings waving slightly in the stiff breeze as it came in to land.

They drove around to the Jet59 entrance and were waved in by the security guard who looked even less interested than he had the last time they were here.

"Honestly, why bother?" Moore said as she navigated around the compound pulling up right outside the small office block.

In the reception area, Mr Davern was duly summoned and appeared a few moments later, looking anxious.

"Good morning, Sergeant. What can we do for you this morning?"

"Good morning, Mr Davern. We'd like to have a chat with the team that Tony Phelan worked with, please. We have some additional questions to ask."

"It's not very convenient, Sergeant. They've only just clocked on, and they are light-handed. We haven't been able to get a replacement for poor Tony yet. It's also a very busy time for us. Ryanair's first wave is coming back in, and they need a quick turnaround."

"Murder isn't very convenient, Mr Davern," Moore said and paused while it sunk in with the recalcitrant manager.

"Well, I suppose you could go around with them as they do their stuff. It's a bit irregular, but if you don't get in the way."

"We won't."

Davern led the two detectives out through a maze of narrow corridors and passages until they reached a stout grey metal door. He used his plastic card to spring the lock, and then ushered Moore and Lawler out into the yard where Joe Donnelly was just topping off his truck with jet fuel.

Davern explained the arrangements to Joe, who looked most uneasy but had little choice in the matter.

The fuel truck that Joe was driving was a double cab affair, and Moore sat in the front beside him, while Wilkinson sat in behind with Joe's helper – Cathal. Cathal was much younger, and Joe explained that he was still learning the ropes. They drove out through the gates of the compound and across the apron towards a row of five Ryanair aircraft.

"We'll do the Stansted one first, Cathal, then we'll tackle the Barcelona one and that should leave us just enough for the Tenerife. Have you got the registration numbers there?"

"The Stansted is X-Ray Yankee, and it's on stand Delta one-four-one."

Joe picked up the microphone attached to a radio set fitted into the dashboard of the truck.

"Ryanair ground ops, this is Joe. Can you confirm your Stansted is X-Ray Yankee on stand Delta one-four-one?"

"Affirmative, Joe. How long will you be?"

"Ten minutes max. Thanks."

"Great. Give me a call when you're done, will ya?"

"Roger that," Joe said and replaced the instrument.

"So, tell me, Joe, how well did you know Tony Phelan then?" Moore asked.

"We had worked together here for years and years. Tony was a good bloke. Very steady and a hard worker too."

"Can you think of anyone who might have wanted to harm him at all?"

"Definitely not. He kept himself to himself. Never got up anyone's nose, except for Davern of course. They didn't like each other."

"What was the problem?"

"When Davern came in, he wanted to change things. He was all talk of productivity and targets, all that shite. Take today, for instance. In the old days, you fuelled one plane at a time, and in between you often got a break for a cuppa. Not anymore. Now we run around like blue-arsed flies all day. Tony didn't like it, and let Davern know what he could do with his clipboard. He was thinking of chucking it in and getting a nice quiet job as a security guard somewhere around here."

"But surely that was just a symptom of the place getting busier?" Wilkinson said from the back seat.

"It wasn't just that. Davern wasn't nice about it. He threatened us all with the sack if we didn't jump to his tune. We have our own way of doing things, and it worked well for years. But he soon backed down when we threatened to go on strike."

Moore processed this and thought to herself that the management hadn't backed down much, as they were going to fill up three planes on this particular trip, but she decided not to provoke the man with her observations.

Joe arrived at the first aircraft and pulled the fuel truck in beside the left wing, away from where the baggage handlers were furiously manhandling bags on and off. Moore had heard that Ryanair had received training from Formula One pit stop crews in order to meet the rapid turnaround times that allowed the company to fit in two extra flights each day, maximising utilization of the aircraft.

"You lot stay here," Donnelly said as he climbed down from his vehicle and set about connecting up the hose to the underside of the plane's wing.

"What do you reckon?" Moore said to Wilkinson when they were on their own again.

"Not much, Sarge. Phelan clearly didn't get on with the boss, but I doubt if Davern shot him, or had him shot."

"Na, me neither. But someone shot the poor bugger."

"What now?" Wilkinson said.

"Let's just stay with them for a while longer. Donnelly looked very jumpy when we arrived. If you get a chance, can you get onto the station and ask someone to look Joe Donnelly up. See if he has form for anything? I'm going to rattle him a bit and see what happens."

Moore didn't get much of a chance to talk to Joe as they serviced the remaining two aircraft. When they were doing the last one, she alighted from the lorry and hung about on the tarmac as the plane was being fuelled, but Joe was busy, and they couldn't really talk with all the aircraft engine noise from other planes coming and going.

When the job was done and they were on their way back to the depot, Moore started her questioning again.

"So, Joe, did you and Tony ever have any arguments?"

"I told you, he was a very private man. Sure, we sometimes disagreed about stuff, but it was all good humoured."

"Did you know he was stealing stuff from the planes?"

"Feck off. You needn't come around here spreading that kind of malicious gossip. It's not right. I'd be careful if I was you," Donnelly said.

"Oh. Why's that?"

Donnelly said nothing, but his face had reddened noticeably, and he was driving more aggressively.

"Where do you live, Joe?"

"On the Malahide Road. One of those little cottages near Woodies. Why?"

"Just routine, that's all."

Wilkinson had made a mental note of Joe Donnelly's address, so that he could check the man out when he got the opportunity.

Back in the Jet59 yard, Moore and Wilkinson left Donnelly and his mate to it. They didn't bother going back into the office to see Davern. As they walked back to their car, Wilkinson was on the phone.

"Donnelly is in the system, OK. But it's from a long time ago. A bit of drunk and disorderly, and he took a swipe at a uniformed Garda, but he was just bound over by the judge. That's it," Wilkinson said.

"Hmm. OK. Hardly a master criminal then. Still, he was definitely jumpy. Let's see how Inspector Burke has been getting on with his missing American."

Chapter Seventeen

It was nearing the end of Joe Donnelly's shift at eight-twenty. The China Skies freighter had landed and been unloaded, and the few pallets of foodstuffs and some high-end fashion goods destined for Shanghai had been placed on board. To keep the aircraft in trim for the next leg of its journey, the cargo was secured in the centre of the plane above the wings. The flight would go back via Schiphol in the Netherlands where the cargo deck would be filled with several more pallets of exports for the long trek back to China.

The crew had gone indoors to have their meal, so the aircraft was left unmanned.

Joe got one of the more senior men and called him over to a quiet spot in the yard.

"Right. Let's get yer man and put him on board. Bring a few tie wraps and some more duct tape. Oh, and I suppose we'd better give the fecker some more water. C'mon, we haven't got long."

The two men retrieved Guy Anderson from the container in which he had spent almost twenty-four hours. He was very subdued, but still managed to put up a bit of a fight as he was shoved into the back of the old van and driven away.

Making sure no one was watching, Joe and his mate manhandled the American into the Airbus. They slid past the freight and took Anderson to the rear of the plane where they manacled him to the side wall where fastenings to secure cargo had been conveniently placed.

"That'll do ye, now. Have a great time in China!" Donnelly said as the two left the plane again and scurried back to the fuel depot.

* * *

"China Skies seven-zero-five requesting engine start," the pilot said into the microphone when the plane had been closed up and prepared for its journey.

"China seven-zero-five, clear to start. When ready, follow the Ryanair 737 to the holding point of runway two-eight. Hold short," the controller responded.

"Roger, China seven-zero-five. Holding point for two-eight."

In the back of the aircraft, Guy Anderson was orienting himself to his new situation. Fortunately, the lights on the cargo deck had been left on, so he could see his grim surroundings quite clearly. He was firmly attached to the side wall of the machine, and he figured his chances of freeing himself without serious injury were slight. In all his time working for the Department of Defense, Anderson had been in some tight spots, but he never thought that a trip to Ireland – considered to be a friendly and safe country by the Americans – would end like this.

As he cast around looking for some way – any way – to improve his position, his eyes fell upon something that might yet save him. There, wedged into the rails that the cargo pallets travelled along, was a small, orange, gas cigarette lighter. It must have been dropped by one of the loaders at some stage. Unfortunately, Anderson had no way of knowing if there was any fuel in it, or if it had been discarded because it was empty. But if he could manage to retrieve it, he might be able to use it to his advantage.

* * *

"China seven-zero-five, line up and wait at runway two-eight," the Dublin air traffic controller said.

"Line up and wait, China seven-zero-five," the pilot repeated.

A few moments later, the controller transmitted again, "China seven-zero-five, cleared take-off runway two-eight. Liffey one Alpha departure. Roll now, please."

"China seven-zero-five rolling."

Inside the aircraft, Anderson heard the huge engines spooling up, and then felt the surge as the machine accelerated down the runway, rotated, and became airborne.

Anderson contorted his body this way and that, and finally managed to release the little orange lighter from where it had lodged in the aircraft's floor. He used his feet to move it towards his manacled hands, and after a lot of straining, managed to get the lighter into his grip.

He flicked the little wheel at the back of the thing and was gratified to see a small yellow flame emerge. He didn't know how much fuel was left in the lighter, so he had to use whatever there was sparingly. He managed to bend his wrist around so that he could burn through the tie wrap tethering his right hand. It hurt like hell, as the little flame scorched his skin, but soon the plastic turned black, stretched and gave way. With his right hand free, he repeated the procedure on the rest of his bindings, and soon he was completely untethered. He ripped the duct tape off his face, which was very painful, but at least he was now free.

Anderson had to decide what to do next. He could probably barge onto the flight deck and tell the flight crew of his plight, but that might not go well. He had heard of situations where the crew of some of these planes were actually armed with low-velocity pistols or tasers, and he didn't fancy making his situation worse.

He decided on another tactic.

* * *

Inside the cockpit, the captain had completed the right-hand turn that would take the plane out over the Irish Sea to Wallasey, where they would get further clearance on into Amsterdam. On the panel in front of him, a red flag appeared in the display, and at the same time a claxon sounded loudly in the cockpit.

The pilot remained cool, but knew that the situation could deteriorate very quickly if indeed there was a fire on board.

"See if you can see anything down the back, will you, Huan?" he said to his first officer who was undoing his seatbelt and climbing out of his seat.

The young co-pilot opened the cockpit door, and immediately smelled burning and saw that the back of the plane was filling with white smoke.

Anderson poured the remains of the water he had been given to drink onto the smouldering embers of paper that he had ripped off one of the cargo pallets, and made even more smoke.

Back in the cockpit, the pilot wasted no time.

"Mayday, mayday, China seven-zero-five. Fire on board. Request immediate return to Dublin for emergency landing."

"Roger, China seven-zero-five. Turn right onto two-two-zero to intercept the localizer, and cleared straight in for two-eight. Do you require ground assistance?"

"Roger that, Dublin. Please roll the fire appliances."

The controller made the call to the fire station at the airport, and was back on the radio almost at once.

"China seven-zero-five, after landing, if you can, vacate the runway at bravo five and stop on the taxiway. We will have fire crew there waiting."

"China seven-zero-five, roger, vacate bravo five, then dead stop."

Six minutes later the wheels of the giant machine touched down on Dublin's runway two-eight. The pilot could see the red fire engines waiting off to the side of the runway with their blue lights flashing and, as directed, he turned off at taxiway B5 and bought his machine to a standstill. Ladders were put up to the side of the plane while the front and rear doors were opened, and firemen raced up and into the aircraft carrying hoses, expecting the worst.

It soon became clear that while there was a lot of smoke, there didn't appear to be any actual fire, and when Guy Anderson emerged from the fog, coughing, spluttering and staggering around, the men from the emergency services got quite a fright.

* * *

Inspector Aidan Burke and Detective Dónal Lawler were in The Boot Inn, questioning the barman and the few patrons about the white GoCar vehicle that had been abandoned outside.

Earlier, Burke had received a call from Gardaí in Swords telling him that the company had been in touch to say that one of their vehicles was parked up near the pub, and that the renter, a Mr Guy Anderson, had seemingly decided on a different form of transport to continue his journey.

The sergeant in Swords had been alerted by email that Anderson was being sought, and had joined the dots, causing him to call in the cavalry from Store Street.

When Burke took the call from the Airport Police, he collected Lawler, and they drove on up to the airport.

When they got to the Airport Police offices, Anderson was seated, tucking into a thickly cut sandwich and a cup of strong coffee. He looked a mess. His clothes were badly stained, and his face was covered in soot, but apart from the obvious signs, he didn't appear to have come to any great harm.

* * *

"I need you to release this man into my custody, sir." Burke said, addressing the Chief Airport Police Officer who had been sent for when Anderson had been brought in from the China Skies plane.

"Eh, not so fast now, Inspector. Apart from the criminal charges, there's the little matter of the expenses. It costs a lot of money to bring an aircraft back like that, and then there's the firemen's charges, not to mention our own. It could mount up to a fair few thousand euros when all that's added up."

"May I have a word in private, please, sir?"

The two men went outside the room and stood in the corridor. Burke explained to the officer about who exactly their prisoner was, and suggested that in order to avoid a more serious international incident, it would be best if Burke just took him away.

"After all, the man was assaulted on the edge of the airport, and I can promise you he didn't put himself on board that aircraft and tie himself up like that," Burke said.

"I see what you mean. Has he any idea who attacked him?"

"We haven't got that far yet, but if I can just get him back into town, I'm sure we will be able to get to the bottom of it. So, am I OK to take him off your hands then?"

The Airport Police Chief wasn't entirely happy, but when Burke gave him an undertaking that any costs would be met by the American Department of Defense, the man relented and told Burke to get him out of there before he changed his mind.

Chapter Eighteen

When Burke, Lawler and Anderson were driving away in Burke's car, Burke opened up the conversation.

"Right. Well, we'd better get you back to your hotel, Guy. You need to get cleaned up, and you're probably starving too. But I don't want any more of your fancy antics, now, do you hear? From now on, we work together, OK? You're messing with some pretty nasty types from what I can see."

"Yes, OK. I hear you," Anderson said.

"That was a good trick with the fire. If you hadn't managed to do that, you'd have ended up in Shanghai with no papers, and God knows what would have happened to you," Lawler said.

"Don't rub it in. And the bastards took my phone. I'd only just got the damn thing!"

"Never mind. Those are ten a penny. Look, can you be in the station in Store Street at nine in the morning? Then we'll see if we can find out who took you and why."

"Yes, sure. No problem."

* * *

Burke and Moore arrived into work the following morning at almost exactly the same time. Burke asked Moore to come into his office, and he told her the story of what had taken place out at the airport the previous night.

"Maybe that will put manners on him. What was he doing out at the pub anyway?"

"He didn't say, but my guess is he was trying to recruit a replacement for Tony Phelan," Burke said.

"Are you serious? Jesus! Do you think you've managed to rein him in a bit?"

"Who knows. What about you, anyway?"

"It's funny. We were out at the airport earlier interviewing Joe Donnelly. Do you think it was him that lifted the Yank?"

"He says he didn't get a proper look at the men that attacked him. But Donnelly fits the description in terms of height," Burke said.

"I think we need another chat with Mr Donnelly, don't you?"

"Yes, I do, but all in good time."

"By the way, boss, I've been thinking about the fire at Phelan's house," Moore said.

"Oh yeah. And?"

"Well, why do you think the person who killed Phelan set the house on fire? After all, he was definitely dead, and there was no evidence that needed covering up, as far as we could see."

"Just being thorough, I guess," Burke said.

"Mmm... I'm not so sure. It seems a bit odd to me."

"So, what do you want to do about it?" Burke said.

"Leave it with me. What's happening today, anyway?"

"Anderson is coming in at nine, and we're going to get a bit more from him about what he was doing and who he was meeting in The Boot Inn. Then we might call on Mr Donnelly and have a little chat. What do you think?"

"Sounds like a plan. Let me know when he gets here. I don't want to miss this!"

* * *

Wilkinson was at his desk when Moore arrived back from her meeting with Burke.

"Hi, Rob. Listen, will you do something for me today?" Moore said.

"Sure. What's on your mind?"

"Can you get onto that estate agent that wrote to Tony Phelan – wait – no, better still, go and see them? Find out if they canvassed anyone else on the road, and probe it a bit. See if you can find out what's going on. In particular, see if you can flush out who their interested buyer was."

"Yes, sure. No bother."

Rob Wilkinson went and retrieved the letter that had been found in Phelan's burnt-out house from McBrien Estates.

He called the office, and made an appointment for that morning to speak to the proprietor, Frank McBrien.

As he left the office, he met Guy Anderson coming into the station.

* * *

Burke, Moore and the beleaguered Guy Anderson were seated in Burke's office. Anderson was cleaned up, and looked a lot better than he had the previous evening. Burke was first to speak.

"Ok, Guy. We need you to tell us all about last night, and everything you know about what's going on here. It's obviously more complicated than it looks."

Anderson looked at both detectives for a moment, as if he was processing exactly how to proceed.

"OK, guys, listen, I'm sorry to say I haven't been entirely up front with you folks. You're right, there is more to it."

Moore looked briefly at Burke and then said, "Go on."

"Well, you know that Tony Phelan was taking a few micro-chips out of some of the consignments from Presswell Exacta and bringing them over to us. Our guys got to analysing exactly what these chips were programmed to do, and I can tell you, they got quite a surprise. Not to put too fine a point on it, the chips, which we believe were destined for European and American communication devices, had some additional functionality built in. Our guys are still working on it to see just exactly what it does, but it looks like it's grade A spyware. They need another few batches of chips to enable them to check it out more thoroughly."

"So, what you're saying is that you needed to recruit a replacement for Tony – hence your clandestine meeting with the fuelling crew last night at The Boot Inn," Moore said.

Anderson looked down at the floor and said nothing.

"But why would they have you jumped, then?" Burke said.

"Search me. It may not have had anything to do with the guys from Jet59. Possibly just an unpleasant coincidence," Anderson said.

"Not when you ended up as extra freight en route to Shanghai. I don't think so," Moore said.

"Oh, yeah, and by the way, did you notice that there are two rows of passenger seats right up at the front of that aircraft, just behind the main door?" Anderson said.

"No. I didn't spot that," Moore said.

"I don't think that is totally unusual. Freighters often have a small number of seats for ferrying crew and the like," Burke said.

"So, what do we do now?" Anderson said.

"I have to spend some time trying to get you off the very serious charge of setting fire to an aircraft, for starters. Fiona, can you spend some time with Guy here and see if you can work up some kind of plan? Later, when I've done some magic with our Superintendent Heffernan, I'll collect you and we'll go out and have another word with Joe Donnelly."

"Right, boss. C'mon, Guy, let's move to my desk."

* * *

"We need to get back to Presswell. That's where the answer lies," Anderson said.

"That's not going to be easy. The place is harder to get into than a tin of sardines, and the owner of the place is as closed as a clam! I don't think a full-frontal approach will do in this case."

"What we need is some bait, right?" Anderson quipped.

"Ha ha, very funny. But you might have something there, Guy. Let's think about that for a while and see if anything nice and devious comes to mind."

Chapter Nineteen

"Mr McBrien? My name is Detective Sergeant Robert Wilkinson. I spoke to your assistant earlier."

"Ah, yes. Please, come into my office."

The office was absolutely tiny. It sat at the back of the small shop on Fairview Strand from where McBrien plied his trade. The place was bright enough, and cleanly furnished with modern equipment, desks and chairs, and the entire room was painted dazzling white to give the impression that it was bigger than it really was.

Wilkinson had noted the window display which was made up of four columns of five vertical A4-sized frames with properties of various kinds offered for sale. Only two had 'Sale Agreed' stamped at an angle in red across the top left corner. Most of the properties were humble houses in the local area which Wilkinson assumed had at one stage been owned by Dublin City Council. 'Corpo houses', as they were known back in the day.

The premises sported two undersized white melamine desks just inside the door, with a pretty blonde in her twenties seated at one of them. The other desk was unoccupied.

When Wilkinson had squeezed himself into McBrien's office and just managed to close the sliding half-glass door behind him, he sat down in one of the two visitors' chairs and tucked his knees under the front of McBrien's desk.

"How can I help you, Detective?"

Wilkinson took the letter that had been retrieved from Tony Phelan's house out and unfolded it, presenting it to the auctioneer.

"I was wondering if you could tell me anything about this, Mr McBrien?"

McBrien studied the crumpled and slightly charred page for a moment.

"Where did you get this?"

"Can you tell me if you regularly send out this type of correspondence, or would it have been at the behest of a specific client?"

"Oh, no, we don't send out fishing letters at all. It would be too costly, and the return on them is abysmal in any case. No, this would have been on behalf of a client," McBrien said.

"May I ask the client's name?"

"Gosh. I don't know. It's quite some time ago. I'm afraid I don't recall."

Wilkinson was a shrewd observer of people, and he knew by the man's body language when he was being fed a line.

"I wonder if your assistant would remember then?" Wilkinson persisted.

"No, I'm afraid not. Janet has only been with us a few months. She's very good, but she wasn't here when this was sent out."

"Mr McBrien, this is important. We need to know the name and nature of the person who was keen to buy Tony Phelan's house. You will have seen in the papers that the man was murdered, and his house burnt down. We need to follow up on even the flimsiest leads. Can you find out for me who was behind your enquiry?"

"Gosh, yes, I did read about that. I'm sorry, but I didn't make the connection until you mentioned it. Look, as you can see, we don't have a lot of room here for filing and the like. I keep all the old files in storage boxes at my home. Why don't I have a look there this evening and see if I can dig it out? I can call you tomorrow and let you know."

"Very well, that would be most helpful. I'll give you my details and you can call me or email me when you have found it. But let me stress again that this is urgent, Mr McBrien, so tomorrow would be good," Wilkinson said.

"Yes, yes, of course."

Wilkinson wrote his contact details down on a sheet of paper for the estate agent. He didn't want to give him his business card revealing that he was attached to the fraud squad. As he squirmed about trying to free himself from the cramped quarters, he chatted to McBrien, and navigated his way back to the public office.

"How's business anyway? Selling many these days?"

"A few. We're not a very big outfit, as you can see, and we have very low overheads, so as long as we can keep things ticking over, that's all we need. Are you a homeowner yourself, Mr Wilkinson?"

"Ever the estate agent, eh, Mr McBrien? I'm fine, thanks. Give me a call tomorrow then." And with that, he was gone.

When Wilkinson left, McBrien went into his office and slid the door closed. He sat down and dialled a number from his desk phone.

"Paul? It's Frank. We may have a problem."

* * *

Wilkinson wasn't entirely happy with the short interview with Frank McBrien. As he got back into his car, he was mulling it over. It was a nice day. There might be some showers later, but for now it was sunny, with just a few menacing grey clouds moving slowly in from the west. Wilkinson realised he was quite near the site of the murder and fire in Fairview. He remembered a wily old detective telling him once that he used to revisit the scene of a murder some time after the event, and often picked up clues that had been missed at the start of the investigation.

He decided to drive up to the Malahide road; he pulled his car in just past the burnt-out hulk of Tony Phelan's house and got out. He walked back to the property and went into the small front garden which was rapidly becoming overgrown. He looked at the poor old place, hoping for inspiration, but nothing came to him. He left the garden again, and walked around to the side of the property, into the laneway that ran up along the boundary formed by the side wall of the house. The lane finished in line with Phelan's back garden where a dark green metal gate with vertical rungs stood open. Wilkinson went through and found himself in a wide expanse of grassed area with the grey concrete buildings of a school some three hundred metres away. There was a rough path etched into the grass that people had clearly used as a shortcut out onto the road at the far side of the school.

Wilkinson walked along the path towards the buildings. As he got near to the school, he noticed that the landscape was being properly tended. Oval beds with colourful blooms in yellow and orange sprouted from the ground, and the edges were neat with no sign of weeds anywhere in sight.

Well over to the right, Wilkinson spotted a man in overalls with a wheelbarrow full of tools beside him. The man was bent over tending to the vegetation and didn't see Wilkinson approaching.

"Good morning," he said, startling the man.

"Jesus, you gave me a fright," the man said, standing up rather stiffly.

He was probably in his sixties, and had that rugged brown skin that people who spend their lives largely outdoors get. He had a cloth cap on his head, with wisps of greasy grey hair protruding, mostly at the back.

"Sorry, I didn't mean to startle you. You have these beds in terrific order. Do you work here full-time?"

"I do indeed. The Christian Brothers are right fussy about the place. But in the summer, some of the lads give me a hand cutting the grass and doing some of the heavy lifting. I'm not as young as I used to be," he said with a wry smile.

"I noticed that down the back there by the lane is not as well kept as the rest of the place. What's the story?" Wilkinson said.

"Ah, sure, aren't they trying to sell that for building? But there's some problem over access. I don't know the details, I just heard them talking about it in the kitchens," the old man said.

"Why do they want to sell it? I thought these religious orders wanted to keep all the land they could."

"I think they want to build a new block of classrooms up here at the side of the old place. They have some of the students in temporary buildings, and they're not suitable, or so they say. And the old building needs a lot of maintenance too. Parts of it are falling down with the damp. They reckon if they sell off that back field, it will fund all of that."

"But they'll not get much for it without the access, surely."

"Ah look, what do I know. I'm just a groundsman. What's your interest anyway?"

"I'm with the Gardaí. We're investigating the death of the man that lived in the house beside the lane."

"Terrible business. I hear he was shot as well," the man said, taking off his cap and scratching his scalp.

"Did you know him at all?"

"No, I didn't. But it's still an awful business. We're not used to that kind of thing around here. Not at all."

"Do you live nearby yourself?"

"I do indeed. Don't they have me in the gate lodge. It's grand, but I'm always on duty when something goes wrong. At least the commute is quick," the old timer said, smirking.

"Ha, yes, I see what you mean. Well, I must be away now. It was good to chat to you. Keep up the good work."

"All the best," the man said, returning his attention to the flower bed.

Chapter Twenty

Superintendent Jerome Heffernan was in a grim mood when Burke was shown into his office. There was none of the usual offer of refreshments, and Burke was greeted by the single word instruction, "Sit."

He sat down in the chair facing his boss, and waited. Heffernan continued to read some papers that he had in front of him on his otherwise clear desk. Burke recognised the tactic and waited patiently for what he knew was to come.

After what seemed like an age, the superintendent looked up.

"Well?" Heffernan said.

"This is worse than I thought," Burke said to himself.

"Sir?" he said tentatively.

"Don't 'sir' me. I'm not in the mood. You know bloody well why you're here."

Burke went on to explain what they knew so far. He tried to play down the antics of the visiting American as best he could, but his boss wasn't satisfied.

"What you're telling me, Inspector, is that you haven't a fucking clue who killed Phelan and set fire to his house. There's a renegade Yankee running around our town like it was the Wild West, and you're about to start World War Three with the Chinese. Is that it?"

"Not quite, sir. We're following some definite leads on the murder, and we're working closely with the American now. I've reined him in. We won't have any more bother from that quarter."

"Hmph. I should bloody well hope not. I have the Department onto me every few hours asking what's going on, and I have shag all to tell them. I need something soon, Aidan. Something juicy to keep the feckers quiet. Otherwise we'll all be back working speed cameras on the M50."

"I hear you, sir. Give me another twenty-four hours, and I should have something more positive to tell you."

"Jesus, Aidan, don't let me down on this one. Now away with ye, and do some bloody detecting!"

* * *

Burke assembled the entire team in the main office when he got back from his meeting with Heffernan.

"Right, listen up. The boss is hopping mad, but only because he's getting it in the neck from just about everyone. We need to step up a gear. Firstly, Guy, I need your word that you will work with us all the way and not go off on some daft solo mission to put the world to rights."

"That's a given, Inspector. I've learned my lesson. Your patch – your party. What can I do to help?"

"I want you to get onto your people in Shanghai. Quietly, though. I'll give you the details of the weapon that was used to kill Phelan, and I want you to find out everything you can about it. Who uses this kind of stuff, OK?"

"Yeah, sure. I'm on it. Can I go and make a few calls before they shut down for the night?"

"Yes. You can use my office. Fiona, can you email Guy the details of the gun?"

"Sure," Moore said, swivelling around to her desktop PC.

"Then you and me are going back out to the airport. I want to talk to Joe Donnelly," Burke said looking at Moore.

"Where's Rob Wilkinson?" Burke said.

"He's out chasing up that letter that Tony Phelan got about his house. He should be back soon," Lawler said.

"When he gets back, I want to know what, if anything, he found out."

"Right, boss," Lawler said.

"Now, we need someone to go and put the fear of God into Flanagan from Presswell. That would be you, Dónal. I don't care how rough you have to get – we need to find out exactly what's going on there. I want him scared. So scared that, if necessary, he will agree to help us with something. Understood?"

"Yes, sir. I might bring a dog handler and a nice unfriendly German shepherd with me for effect. What do you reckon?"

"Excellent idea. And don't take any shit from him. He may well have connections, but so have we!"

* * *

When Burke had finished setting the team off in various directions, he and Fiona Moore drove back out to the airport. This time, they took a brightly-coloured squad car from the pool, and as they approached the gates of the Jet59 compound, Moore put on the blue lights.

The so-called security guard nodded as they drove in, and as they pulled up in front of the building, they spotted Joe Donnelly lumbering across towards one of the fuelling trucks.

Moore hopped out and approached the man.

"Mr Donnelly, we need a word."

"Now is not a good time, Sergeant, I'm busy. I have to fuel up two Ryanair planes, and they won't thank me if they are delayed."

"OK, well then maybe we had better do this at the Garda station. Do I have to arrest you?" Moore said, fondling a pair of handcuffs she had taken from her jacket pocket.

Donnelly looked at her straight in the eye for a moment, and turned to a colleague who had been walking out of the building with him.

"Cathal, can you do these two on your own?"

Cathal just nodded, walked on and climbed aboard the truck.

Moore and Donnelly sat into the back seat of the Hyundai squad car.

"What's all this about?" Donnelly said.

"We believe you may have been involved in the assault and kidnap of an American citizen outside The Boot Inn the other night," Burke said.

"You have no proof that it was me," Donnelly said, and went on, "besides, that fecker was responsible for Tony getting himself killed, so he got what he deserved."

"In your own words, you have no proof that he had anything to do with Tony's death. And you need to leave the police work to us. Besides, he was on his way out here to do you a favour," Moore said.

"Favour, was it? Not bloody likely!"

"Listen, Joe, are you really interested in bringing Tony Phelan's killer to justice – proper justice, not some vigilante nonsense?" Burke said.

"What do you mean?"

"Look, we'll level with you. Your mate Tony was doing a bit of moonlighting. He was helping himself to some micro-chips out of those consignments that are delivered to the China Skies freighter now and then."

"But that's impossible. The stuff they deliver in that security van is locked away in strong boxes, and anyway, what would Tony be doing with those yokes? Na, you're wrong."

"We're not wrong, Joe. Tony had a set of keys for the boxes, and he was passing the stuff on to the Americans. He took it with him when he went to the States," Burke said.

Donnelly took a few moments to digest this new information.

"Maybe. But what's all this to do with me?"

"That American that was grabbed out here and put on the plane to Shanghai was actually coming to see if he could find a replacement for Tony. He had nothing to do with Phelan's murder. He just needed someone to carry on with Tony's work."

"Fucking hell! And then I suppose whoever took over would have been bumped off as well. Not feckin likely!"

"Well, Joe, you see, it's not quite as simple as that. We need someone to do what Tony was doing just once more. There's no risk. We have all the bases covered. We'll give you a set of keys for the boxes, and all you have to do is lift, say, a dozen chips out and put in a dozen blanks which we'll give you. Then we'll collect the genuine ones from you a few days later. You'll be perfectly safe," Moore said.

"And if I don't agree?"

"Then we do you for assault and kidnap. Five years – that is if the Americans don't extradite you and send you straight to Guantánamo Bay in a nice new orange jumpsuit," Burke said.

"Fuck you! I don't exactly have much choice, do I?"

"Not really, no. Now give us a day or two to set all this up, and we'll be back in touch. Is there anything else you can tell us, particularly about the comings and goings of that China Skies aircraft?"

Donnelly thought for a moment.

"There is one thing, but it's probably not important. A couple of days before Tony was killed, the plane came in late. I dunno, some shite about air traffic control or something. Anyway, they asked us to expedite the refuelling, so we got out there pronto as soon as she'd docked. When the door was opened, the crew came down the stairs and went inside as usual. There were five of them in all, and they were togged out in the regular black suits, white shirts and white cotton gloves and peaked caps. But a few minutes later, another person disembarked. He was in plain clothes. A small guy, carrying a holdall. We didn't see his face – we were too busy doing the fuel – but he disappeared pretty quickly. We didn't see where he went."

"Was that unusual?"

"Kinda. They quite often have one or two passengers with them, but they are just checking the loading process and they always hang around till it's all done, and then get back on board."

"Did this guy go back with them?" Moore said.

"No, he didn't. We stayed with the plane till the loading was finished in case we had to top it off or take some fuel back, depending on the gross weight of the machine and cargo. That quite often happens. But there was no sign of yer man."

"Hmm. Interesting. Right, Joe. That's us for now. We'll let you get back to work. We'll call you tomorrow or the next day to set this up. OK?"

"I s'pose. But you'll look after me, won't you?"

"Of course!"

* * *

As Burke and Moore were driving back to town, Moore said, "Here's a nice long shot for you. Why don't we see if we can get a list of Chinese citizens who left through Dublin Airport the day after Tony was killed?"

"Jesus. There will be hundreds, if not more. Sounds like a needle in a haystack to me," Burke said.

"Yeah, but we can narrow it down a good bit," Moore said, not wanting to be put off so easily.

"How so?"

"Let's look for someone departing for the UK, with an ultimate destination of Shanghai, probably doing the onward flight with China Skies. My guess would be Manchester or Birmingham. How's that?"

"Hmm... OK. Go for it. Get Wilkinson on it. He's good at that sort of thing."

Moore made the call.

Chapter Twenty-One

Wilkinson told Moore what had transpired when he went to visit Frank McBrien in the little estate agent's office earlier in the day.

"I got the impression he was decidedly jittery. And I went on out to Phelan's house, too. And guess what? You know the field behind the house?" Wilkinson said.

"Yeah, what about it?" Moore said.

"It seems it's ripe for development, but there's an access issue. I spoke to a groundsman out at the school, and he was telling me the Christian Brothers are trying to sell it for building."

"Cripes! Are you thinking what I'm thinking?"

"Exactly, Sarge. If Tony's house was flattened, then with that little laneway to the side and Tony's house demolished – bingo! A hundred new apartments in a prime location. Worth a good few bob, don't you think?" Wilkinson said.

"I'll say. I'll tell the boss later on and see what he says. Any luck with the Chinese guy and the airlines?"

"I'm waiting for them to get back to me. I started with passport control. They had seventy-four Chinese nationals that departed that day. Most were going to either Europe or the USA, but I have the airlines running the names now and when they get a hit on a booking onwards to Shanghai, they'll call me back."

"Great. Let us know as soon as you get anything. Have you heard from Dónal?"

"Sorry, I haven't been watching out for a call. I've been pretty busy with this stuff," Wilkinson said.

"No worries, I'll give him a call myself."

* * *

Detective Dónal Lawler got into the little unmarked white Peugeot van that had arrived at the station.

"Morning, Mick. Thanks for coming around. How's Cesar?"

Cesar was the German shepherd that Mick Tyrrell looked after for the Gardaí. The dog was almost totally black, with just a small blaze of tan fur on his chest. But with a completely black face and dark eyes, he could look very menacing when the occasion demanded, though when the dog was off duty, he was a sweet-natured creature.

Lawler had worked with Tyrrell and Cesar a few times previously and was always mightily impressed with how the two of them operated in total harmony, each one looking out for the other as they ran some fairly serious criminals to ground.

"He's in great form. Glad to be working. What's the story out here anyway?" Tyrrell said.

"I don't think it will be rough. We just need to look as if we mean business. You're both along more for appearance than anything else," Lawler said.

"Aw, shit. And there we were, looking for some action, weren't we, boy?" Tyrrell said to the dog through the metal mesh that separated the front of the van from the canine quarters in the back.

Cesar gave a loud grunt.

They drew the van up to the metal gates at the rear of Unit 22 and all three got out. Cesar was now on high alert, sniffing around diligently to orient himself to his new surroundings.

Lawler had a good look around, and spotted a CCTV camera high up on the side of the building that was moving slowly in an arc, observing the new arrivals. He took his warrant card out and held it up to the camera.

"Police. Open up," he said, hoping that the device was fitted with a microphone.

A tinny voice came back a second later. "Just a moment," it said.

Cesar looked at the camera, tilting his head first one way and then the other, trying to calculate where the strange voice was coming from.

After what seemed like an age, a man in a brown shop coat appeared from inside the building and strolled over to the gates. He opened a small door set into the larger gate, and admitted the two Gardaí and Cesar, who immediately put his nose to the ground, sniffing all around.

"We're here to see Mr Flanagan," Lawler said to the man.

"You're out of luck, I'm afraid. The boss isn't here today. Can anyone else help?" the man said, looking curiously at Cesar, who was extending his range, thanks to the stretchy lead that Tyrrell had attached to his collar.

"When will he be here?" Lawler said.

"Probably tomorrow morning, but we're never sure when exactly he's going to turn up. That way, he keeps us on our toes."

"What's your function here, Mr…?"

"Kelly, Denis Kelly. I'm the warehouseman. I check in the raw materials, organise the shelves and so on, and get the finished goods ready for export."

"Have you worked here long, Mr Kelly?" Lawler said.

"I have indeed. Ten years next month. It's a handy enough job. And Flanagan is OK to work for if you do your job properly."

Cesar had guided Mick Tyrrell across the warehouse floor to where a stack of aluminium crates was piled, one on top of the other. The dog was sniffing eagerly around the boxes, and after a few moments let out a couple of loud barks which echoed chillingly through the metal structure, before sitting down and staring persistently at the pile of containers.

"Dónal, over here," Tyrrell said, nodding his head in the direction of Cesar when he had caught his attention.

"What's in those?" Lawler said to Kelly.

"They're just empties back in from the airport."

Lawler walked over to where Tyrrell and Cesar were standing.

"Could you open the bottom one for me please, Mr Kelly," Lawler said, noting that it was this one that seemed to be holding Cesar's attention.

"They're just empty crates. I told you, they send them back from China so we can re-use them for the next shipment."

Lawler said nothing, and waited.

When it became clear that Lawler wasn't going to relent, Kelly started to take down the boxes, and when the bottom one was exposed, he flipped the catches all along the front and lifted the lid.

Cesar immediately jumped up and stuck his head inside the box. When he took his head back out, he barked several more times, looking up at Tyrrell as if to convey some message that he knew his handler would understand.

"Not quite empty, Mr Kelly," Lawler said as he leaned in himself and spotted a light dusting of white crystalline residue in the corners of the container.

"I think we need to call in some of our colleagues, Mr Kelly. Please ensure that no one leaves the premises until we can have this properly investigated."

Kelly looked sullen.

"I don't know what you think you have found, officer, but I can assure you it has nothing to do with me," Kelly said.

Lawler said nothing. He went outside, out of earshot, and made a call to Aidan Burke back in Store Street. When he had put his boss in the picture, Burke said, "Well done, Dónal. Nice one. I'll get the drug squad out immediately. See if you can find out exactly where Flanagan is today as well. We need to interview him. And thank the dog handler for us too. That was a good call."

"Right, boss. Talk later."

Kelly rather reluctantly showed Lawler where the office was located, and he made his way up a set of metal stairs and through a partially glazed door into a spacious, functional reception area where two girls were seated behind a large oak-coloured desk.

Lawler introduced himself to the two women.

"I need to get a hold of Mr Flanagan, ladies. Can you tell me where he is today?"

The girl nearest to Lawler spoke up. She was in her twenties, and was plain-looking and cheerful.

"He's not in today, I'm afraid. But he'll be here tomorrow," she said with a smile.

"I need to speak to him now. May I have his mobile number?" Lawler said.

"We're under strict instructions not to give that out to anyone, I'm afraid, officer. It would be more than my job is worth. Sorry."

"Look, I can see your point of view, but I need the number. Why don't you just jot it down on a scrap of paper, leave it on your desk, and go to the bathroom. That way you didn't give it to me if anyone is asking, I just went snooping and came across it."

The girl looked at her companion, who just shrugged her shoulders. She wrote the number on a yellow Post-it Note, and stuck it to the desk. When she had got up and was walking away, Lawler reached across and picked it up.

"I'm not going to thank you, because you didn't actually give it to me," he said, smiling, and the girl smiled back.

By the time he got downstairs, two Toyota 4x4 jeeps had arrived with a total of six members of the drugs squad. They were getting suited up, ready for a thorough examination of the premises. Lawler nodded to Mick Tyrrell, and they made their way back outside to the small white van.

Tyrrell gave Cesar a drink of water from a stainless-steel bowl that he always carried in the van and the dog lapped it up enthusiastically. It was also a signal to Cesar that his job was complete for the moment, and Lawler petted the dog's head and complimented him on his excellent work.

"Good boy, Cesar, who's a clever fella then?" Lawler said, bending down to bring his face level with the animal's. Cesar responded warmly, licking Lawler's face, and pawing at his outstretched arm.

After a moment, Mick Tyrrell opened the back of the van, and Cesar hopped up into the cage, settling down quickly for the journey back to base.

On the way back to town in the van, Dónal Lawler relayed the phone number he had been given for Cian Flanagan. Burke said he would get onto it immediately and have Flanagan brought in for questioning.

Chapter Twenty-Two

Burke brought the five of them together late in the afternoon for a status update.

"Right. Let's see what we've got. Rob, what's your story?"

"I got a call back from my new best friend at the airport. They told me that the only passenger that booked a flight to the UK and on to Shanghai the same day we found Phelan's dead body, was a Li Jun. I asked the guy to dig a bit deeper, and he confirmed that Jun had just one piece of cabin baggage. No checked-in stuff at all."

"Hmm... interesting. That could be our man then. Guy, can you give that name to your people and see if anything pops up. You have much greater intelligence than we have on the Far East," Burke said.

"Yeah, sure. Though I guess there could be a lot of guys with the same name out there, but we'll see. Oh, and while I have the floor, I got my guys to do some checking on that weapon you asked about. They told me they were originally military issue, but the military stopped using them about fifteen years ago, and many of the weapons found their way into the hands of a gang of criminals known as the Woo Tee Yang. They specialize in extortion and contract killings, especially overseas."

"Lovely. Just what we need – a Chinese turf war right here in little old Dublin. Thanks, Guy. That's helpful, at least. What about you, Fiona. What have you got?"

Moore retold the group what Wilkinson had found out about the development potential attached to Tony Phelan's house.

"OK," Burke said, "looks like your theory that the two events may not be connected may have some merit, Sergeant. Where to now on this one?"

Wilkinson put his hand up.

"McBrien is to get back to me with details of the client on whose behalf he sent the letter to Tony Phelan. He probably won't, but if he doesn't, I'll go back and lean on him a bit and see what I can get."

"Good man. Stay on it. That could be crucial," Burke said.

Burke went on to tell the little group about Dónal Lawler's visit to Presswell Exacta.

"I have the boys out in Dalkey looking for him. There's no sign of him for now, but my guess is he'll return home later, and then we'll have him. Right, I'll hang on here till Flanagan turns up. You lot get off home, we have a busy day ahead tomorrow," Burke said.

Fiona Moore followed her boss into his office.

"Do you want me to wait too, boss? It could be late enough by the time Flanagan turns up, and it would be better if we both interviewed him, given the circumstances."

"Yeah, OK, thanks. And could we get some food in? I'm starving!"

"Chinese takeaway?" Moore said smiling.

"Ha, very funny. But chips, not rice, OK?"

"But of course!" Moore said, enjoying the banter with her senior officer. It had been a while since they had had any personal time together, and while there was no romantic involvement between them, they did enjoy each other's company.

When Moore had procured a few foil trays of excellent Chinese food from the carry-out place around the corner from the station, they sat into his office and tucked in.

"How's your photography course going?" Burke said between mouthfuls.

"Pretty good, thanks. I've signed up for a weekend away with the group to do some landscape work in County Wicklow before the weather turns nasty. Should be a bit of fun."

"That sounds cool. How many of you are going?"

"I think there's about eight of us enrolled just now, but it's not for a few weeks, so we may get more. The tutor is really good. He's taken some amazing stuff in and around Enniskerry."

Burke's phone rang.

"Burke."

"Inspector, this is Sergeant Walsh out in Dalkey. You were looking for a Mr Flanagan from Glenageary, I believe."

"Yes, that's right, Sergeant. What's the news?"

"Well, we have him here for you. We brought him in about ten minutes ago, but he's not too happy. What do you want us to do with him?"

"Hang on to him there for us. We'll be out in half an hour or so."

"Fair enough. See you then."

* * *

They took Burke's car and drove out of town skirting Sandymount, and on through Booterstown and Blackrock. Then Burke turned down by the coast, and they drove into Seapoint, past the now disused ferry port at Dún Laoghaire, finally reaching the little village of Dalkey known for its gastronomic delights.

They parked outside the Garda station and went in.

Five minutes later, they were seated in an uncomfortably small interview room along with Cian Flanagan and his solicitor who had been hastily summoned by the man. The solicitor, Andrew Green, was a sullen, wiry person with frameless glasses worn on a long face. Despite the hour, Green was wearing a business suit, and had a smart leather briefcase with him, and a jotter for taking notes.

"Well, Mr Flanagan, as I said before, you're a hard man to get hold of. Where have you been all day?"

Green replied on behalf of his client.

"My client's whereabouts are none of your concern, Inspector. Now if you have any genuine questions to ask, let's get on with it."

"OK. Let's. As I am sure you are aware, Mr Flanagan, we had reason to call to your premises earlier today out in Citywest. Whilst conducting enquiries at the site, we came across some evidence of class A drugs in a container that you had recently imported from China. Have you anything to say about that?" Burke said.

Green responded again.

"Inspector, I understand you entered my client's business premises and carried out a search without a warrant. Whatever you think you may have found is meaningless under those circumstances, as you well know."

"Our officers were invited on to your premises by, let me see" – Moore consulted her notes – "a Mr Kelly, the storeman. Fortunately, my men had a dog with them, and the animal made straight for a container in which a residue of white crystalline powder was located. We are having it properly analysed at present, but an on-site test showed indications of cocaine."

Green whispered something in Flanagan's ear, making sure the detectives couldn't overhear.

"Whatever you may have found, Sergeant, I can assure you I know nothing whatever about it. Although I imagine it will turn out to be something quite innocent. Silica perhaps. We use that to ensure the products don't get damp during transit. The humidity at some of the stops on route to China can be very high."

Moore turned to Burke.

"I don't think our drug dogs are trained to react to silicone, Inspector, do you?"

"Bloody nonsense. You think we were born yesterday?" Burke said, unable to contain his vexation at the line being taken by Flanagan and his ultra-smooth lawyer.

"Nevertheless, in the absence of any actual evidence against my client, I think we'll be on our way," Green said, collecting up his papers and tapping them on the table.

Burke's phone pinged. It was a text message from Dónal Lawler saying simply, 'Please call me. Thanks'.

"You'll have to excuse me for a moment, folks. Please don't go anywhere till I come back."

Burke got up and left the room, and once outside called Dónal Lawler.

"Hi. What's up, Dónal?"

"Hello, sir. I have some results back from the lab on that stuff we found out at Presswell. Cocaine. Very pure. Almost certainly from China, according to the chemist."

"I see. Any sign of any more of it anywhere out there?"

"No, sir. But there were some areas we weren't allowed to access. They have clean rooms where part of the chip manufacturing is done, and the lads didn't have the right gear. They're going back tomorrow when they have proper clean suits."

"Right. Have we left someone out there making sure they don't move anything off the premises?"

"Yes, sir. Some of the Gardaí from Tallaght are stationed at the factory."

"Great. Thanks Dónal, that's helpful. See you tomorrow."

Back in the interview room, Burke lost no time in cranking up the tension.

"I can now confirm that the substance found on your premises earlier today is cocaine. And as you are the sole director of the company that occupies the premises, I intend to charge you with the importation of the drug into Ireland," Burke said.

"That's preposterous. It could have been any one of Mr Flanagan's employees, or what about that crowd out at the airport that are up to no good?" Green said.

"Mr Green, we'll be keeping your client in for the night while we continue with our enquiries. Sergeant, would you take Mr Flanagan outside and have him checked in, please."

Flanagan turned to his lawyer.

"Can they do that? I mean, I haven't done anything. For God sake, get me out of here."

"Don't worry, Cian, I'll have you out of here first thing tomorrow. Just play along for now. It will be fine," the lawyer said, but it wasn't him who was going to be spending the night in the cells!

Chapter Twenty-Three

When Burke and Moore got back to Burke's office in the city, there was a message for Burke to call Guy Anderson, and a new mobile number for the man.

"I wonder what he wants?" Moore said. It was now getting on into the evening, they had both had a busy day and were keen to get out of the station.

"I'd better call him. I don't want him thinking we're ignoring him and going off on his own again. He'd probably get himself killed, and then we'd have another murder to solve."

Moore smiled and sat down facing her boss as he made the call.

"Guy? It's Aidan Burke. You were looking for me."

"Thanks for calling, Inspector. May I ask, are you still at the station?"

"Yep, afraid so. What can I do for you?"

"I'd like to come over and have a chat with you, if I may. I've been speaking to some colleagues back in the States, and they want me to explore a particular avenue with you."

"OK. I have Sergeant Moore with me too. C'mon over then."

Fifteen minutes later, Guy Anderson arrived in Burke's office bearing three large cardboard cups of coffee and three donuts that he had purchased from the Café Sol opposite the station.

"Good man, Guy. I'm starving," Moore said when she saw the food.

They sat at Burke's desk, and when the donuts were devoured and half the coffee was gone, Burke opened up the real conversation.

"So, what's on your mind, Guy?"

"My folks back home are very concerned about what's going on with this Presswell Exacta place. They feel that these guys could get up to anything with the Chinese, and they don't like it. Do you think there's any way we could get someone in there to keep an eye on them?"

Moore looked at Burke who nodded imperceptibly.

"There's been a development, Guy," Moore said, and went on to outline recent events.

"Awesome! Do you think Flanagan is importing the stuff?"

"That's what we're trying to find out. But one way or the other, it gives us some leverage. To be honest, it's going to be damn difficult to prove his involvement, unless we find his fingerprints on those boxes – which we won't. He's way too clever for that. As he said himself, it could be any one of his employees, or even the lads out at the airport that are bringing it in. But one way or the other, we need to put a stop to it. There's enough of that shit on the streets of Dublin already without bringing planeloads of it in from bloody China!"

"Interesting. He may well have played right into our hands. Do you think we could go and have a word with Flanagan tonight?"

"God, I don't know, Guy. That's very irregular. He'll want his sleazy solicitor there. But there may be a way. Hold on. I'll make a call."

* * *

Thirty minutes later, Burke pulled the brightly-coloured squad car up to the door of Dalkey Garda station. He went into the building with Moore in tow, leaving Guy Anderson in the back seat of the vehicle. When they got inside, the desk sergeant greeted them and said, "I have your client all ready to go. He's not very happy about it, but I explained that he was just being transferred to a city centre station as we don't have the facilities here to make him comfortable overnight."

"Thanks, Sergeant. Can you fetch him now, and we'll get going?"

Flanagan appeared, and started complaining almost immediately.

"I want my solicitor informed that you're spiriting me away. He should be going with me, by rights."

"That's all taken care of, Mr Flanagan, have no fear. Mr Green will be put in the picture," Burke said.

"Why are you moving me, anyway?"

"We think you'll be more comfortable in Store Street, and it will save us a journey out here in the rush hour tomorrow morning."

Flanagan was ushered down the steps of the Garda station and placed in the back seat of the Hyundai alongside Guy Anderson. Burke introduced the two men, describing Anderson as a colleague from the United States who was helping them with their enquiries into the murder of Tony Phelan.

They were just turning down the narrow little road that would bring them onto the coast at Sandycove when Anderson started talking to Flanagan.

"I hear you're involved in the design and manufacture of micro-chips for the Far Eastern market, Mr Flanagan. Nice business. They must have a terrific appetite for that stuff," Anderson said.

"We do okay."

"It's funny though, my people back home tell me that your chips have a few, shall we say, undisclosed features that make them pretty valuable to your customers."

Flanagan shuffled restlessly in his seat.

"I don't know what you mean," he said.

"Oh, come on now, we're not fools, Flanagan. We know exactly what you're up to, and I can tell you, there are quite a few of my colleagues in the USA that are very unhappy about it. Very unhappy indeed."

"Who is this guy?" Flanagan said to Burke.

Burke didn't respond.

"And I hear you've got yourself into a spot of bother over some drugs too. Bad business that. Carries a pretty heavy sentence in this country, or so I hear."

"Look, what's going on here, Burke? I want my lawyer. This is outrageous!"

Anderson was next to speak.

"Of course, there is a way that we could make all this nastiness disappear for you, Mr Flanagan."

Flanagan said nothing, but Anderson had piqued his interest all the same.

"You see, Uncle Sam would be very grateful if you would allow one of our own technicians to join your team of designers at Presswell Exacta. Call it part of the 'special relationship', if you will. What do you think?"

"And what exactly would this person be doing?"

"Let's just say, he might suggest some slight modifications to your designs – nothing major, you understand. In fact, your customers out east wouldn't even notice anything different."

Flanagan thought about what had been suggested as the car drove along the Rock Road towards Dublin.

"And what if I agree?"

"I think you'll find Inspector Burke here won't have enough evidence to bring charges against you for the importation of illegal drugs, once you give a solemn undertaking that it stops immediately. And my people will be very grateful. We would love to examine how some of your products could be utilized by one or two of our American device manufacturers. It could be very lucrative for you."

Flanagan was warming to the idea.

"I'm not sure our Chinese customers would be too happy if we started dealing with the USA. They would probably get suspicious, and cut us off."

"Don't worry about that. We can route the business through Singapore. We have a few companies set up out there. You could even use China Skies to deliver the goods."

"And if I don't agree?"

"Simple. We close down your factory and extradite you to the USA on charges of espionage. Have you seen what we do to foreign spies in America these days? It's not pretty."

Flanagan remained silent for quite a while as they motored back towards the city.

Anderson and the two detectives stayed quiet too. Somewhere along the way, they had learned that the next person to speak in these situations usually lost the argument. They weren't disappointed.

As the car met the much busier traffic on the quays, Flanagan spoke up.

"OK, then. I agree. What happens now?"

Burke was the next to speak.

"We release you tomorrow morning without charge, and you go back to work. You sort out the drugs thing for us, and then Mr Anderson will be in touch to introduce you to your new employee. You'll be needing more staff in any case as your business grows with your new contracts. And if you ever breathe a word about any of this to anyone, well, I'll leave that to your imagination. And of course, if you don't follow through with what we have discussed, we'll come after you. Oh, and by the way, this conversation never happened."

Chapter Twenty-Four

Robert Wilkinson had, unsurprisingly, heard nothing from Frank McBrien. He decided he had better call in again and put a bit of pressure on the man. But before driving out to Fairview, he logged onto the Dublin City Council website to have a look at the town plan for the area around Marino.

The website wasn't the easiest to navigate. It was as if the Council didn't really want all and sundry looking at the plans, possibly for fear of protests which seemed to pop up any time there was a plan for anything new these days. But there was a dire shortage of housing in Dublin, and the authorities were doing whatever they could, albeit at their own rather relaxed pace, encouraging new schemes to ease the pressure on their own paltry supply of habitable properties.

Dublin, like many cities across the UK and Ireland, had got caught up in the right-to-buy wave that swept through during the 1980s, reducing the number of state-owned properties to a fraction of what it had been in earlier decades. Economically, the notion looked good on paper, but as time went by, the policy saw more and more people at the lower end of the economic spectrum becoming homeless, and for whatever reason, successive governments appeared to be unable to reverse the trend.

Wilkinson brought up the zoning map of the area, and saw that the land behind Tony Phelan's house had been re-zoned. In the 2011 development plan, the land belonging to the school had been zoned Z9, a recreational amenity, but in the latest plan it had changed to Z1 – residential.

* * *

Janet, the pretty blonde that worked with McBrien, was seated behind her tiny desk in the estate agent's office when Wilkinson entered.

"Good morning, Janet. Is Mr McBrien in?"

"No, sorry. He's gone to see a client on the southside. He'll be back after lunch, I imagine. Look, I'm just about to make a cup of coffee. Would you like one?"

"Thanks. That's very hospitable. Milk, no sugar."

As Janet got up and side-stepped through to the back of the office where a kettle and a microwave were perched on a narrow shelf, she said, "I'm glad of the company, to be honest. There's very little traffic through here, and it gets a bit boring. Not what I was expecting when I joined."

She busied herself making two mugs of coffee.

"Do you not get out to show the properties at all?" Wilkinson said.

"No. Mr McBrien looks after all that. I just do the paperwork and keep the website updated. We do sometimes get some people in, but they don't stay long. They usually just pick up a leaflet."

Janet handed Wilkinson his drink, and the two of them sat down at her desk.

"Are you from round here?" Wilkinson said.

"Me? Oh no. I'm a southsider. I was brought up in Donnybrook and went to school in Muckross. Then I went into the College of Marketing and did a degree. I worked for another estate agents when I had finished, but it was nearly all lettings, and I didn't like the guy that owned it much. He was a bit 'hands-on' if you know what I mean."

"Oh, gosh. That must have been tricky for you."

"It was at first, but I soon got the measure of him. But the job wasn't going anywhere, so I was glad when this opportunity came up."

"Is it just the two of you in the office?" Wilkinson said.

"Mostly. Mrs McBrien comes in on Fridays most weeks just to do the accounts. The office is a little busier then. But the rest of the time it's just us, and quite often just little old me," she said, smiling.

"None of the same old trouble with McBrien, I presume?"

"Oh, no. He's very well behaved."

The two of them drank their coffee in silence for a few more minutes. Before the silence became embarrassing, Wilkinson spoke.

"I was hoping Mr McBrien would have dug out the source of that enquiry on Tony Phelan's property I was asking about. He didn't mention anything to you about it, did he?"

"No, he didn't. But what is it you want to know? I might be able to find it in the system. This thing is pretty ancient, and it looks like the files on here go back years," Janet said pointing at the beige flat-panel monitor on her desk.

Wilkinson went on to explain about the letter that had been recovered from Phelan's house.

"Give me a minute, I'll have a look."

Janet ran the mouse around on her desk and clicked a few keys.

"Yes, here we are. We wrote to Mr Phelan about possible interest in the acquisition of his property."

"Does it say who initiated the enquiry?"

"Hang on." Janet tapped the keyboard again.

"Yep! Got it. Paul Glinn. If I remember rightly, he's a builder. I've seen other transactions on the system involving site purchases and land deals. Sad, isn't it? When I get really fed up, I browse through the old files just for something to do," she said, smiling.

"That's great, Janet. Are there contact details for Glinn?"

"Yes." Janet reached for a shorthand notebook and wrote down the details she was looking at on the screen. She tore off the page and handed it to Wilkinson.

"Thanks a lot. That's really helpful," Wilkinson said, and started to get up.

"That's right. Now that you've got what you wanted, just get up and leave me all alone. Typical man!" she said with a twinkle in her eye.

"Well, no, actually. I was wondering if you'd like to come out for a drink, or maybe some grub some evening after work?"

"Hmm... OK. That would be nice. On one condition, though."

"What's that?"

"You don't interrogate me about this place."

"Deal! I'll call you in a day or two. May I have your number?"

Janet gave him one of the business cards that was parked in a little plastic container on her desk.

"Thanks. Catch you later, and thanks for the coffee and the chat."

"See ya!" she said, her humour much improved.

* * *

Wilkinson drove back to the station before calling Paul Glinn. He didn't want Janet to see him making the call, and in any case, he knew that all calls made from the station's landlines were recorded, which could be useful in this particular case.

The number Janet had given him was a mobile number, though he also had an address. Sitting at his desk in the open plan, he made the call.

The phone was answered quite promptly, but there was a massive amount of background noise, and Glinn could barely hear what Wilkinson was saying.

"What? Sorry, who did you say?" Glinn said, as the cacophony continued in the background.

"Detective Robert Wilkinson. Look, this is hopeless. Can we meet somewhere?"

"Sorry, I can't hear you. Could you come and meet me, maybe?" Glinn said.

"Where are you now?" Wilkinson blared down the phone, causing the others in the office to look up from their work.

"Sandymount Green. You'll see the big hoarding. I'll be here for another hour." And the line went dead.

* * *

Wilkinson drove out to Sandymount Green. Just at the far side from the main road, a massive hoarding was wrapped around a site where a number of shops and little cottages had been demolished. A picture of the development was fixed to the outside of the hoarding, holding out the promise of twelve luxury apartments with underfloor heating, en-suite bedrooms and state-of-the-art kitchens.

'Glinn Construction' was plastered across the grey plywood in enormous navy-blue letters.

Wilkinson parked up and strolled over to the double gates where a concrete lorry was reversing in to deposit its load. A man in a high-viz jacket and a bright yellow hard hat stood overseeing the manoeuvre, smoking a cigarette.

"Hi. I'm looking for Paul Glinn," Wilkinson said to the man.

"He was here a minute ago. Oh, look, there he is, over by the portacabin," the man said, gesturing to a small grey temporary office at the far side of the site, "but you can't come in without a hard hat. Hang on a sec, I'll get you one."

The man disappeared behind the gates and emerged a moment later holding another rather grubby bright yellow helmet. Wilkinson wondered about the hygiene of the protection he was being offered, but donned the hat in any case. He set off across the soft ground to the cabin.

"Mr Glinn?"

"Yes, how can I help?" Glinn said looking up from his phone.

"I'm Detective Wilkinson, we spoke earlier. Is there somewhere quiet we could have a chat?"

"Sure. Come inside, it's not as noisy. What's on your mind?"

The portacabin had a desk festooned with drawings, books, notepads and several used and unwashed cups, and was not in very good condition. The chairs were the moulded plastic type that came in orange or grey originally, but were now just blackened with dirt. Several pairs of muddy builders' boots were lined up against the wall of the office, and a single fluorescent tube lit the place. Glinn signalled to Wilkinson to take a seat as he sat down himself at the far side of the desk.

"Mr Glinn, I understand you were interested in buying a property in Marino, just behind the school there. It belonged to a Mr Tony Phelan."

"Was I? I don't recall. But we're always on the look-out for development opportunities. It took me six years to put this lot together. There were four separate owners here. Why do you ask?"

"Are you sure you don't recall this particular property? You would have dealt with Frank McBrien at the time."

"I told you, I don't remember. Why is it so important anyway?"

"Mr Phelan's house is at the entrance to lands that have been re-zoned for residential development, but there's an access problem. With Phelan's house out of the way, access would be enabled. The property was burned down recently, and I'm afraid Mr Phelan was inside at the time. He's dead."

"Jesus! I'm sorry to hear that. But I hope you're not accusing me of any involvement in it?" Glinn said.

"I'm not accusing anyone of anything, Mr Glinn. I'm just trying to find out what happened, that's all."

"Why did you come here? I've nothing to do with that place."

"Do you know the land I'm describing?"

"Yes, I do. We looked at it a couple of years ago, but as you say, there's an access problem, so we passed on it. I have enough to be doing focusing on the properties we can actually develop. Was there anything else, Detective?"

"How many men do you have working for you, Mr Glinn?"

"It varies a lot, but just now, around sixty directly employed, and then there are the sub-contractors of course. Why?"

"I wonder if you could let me have a list of their names – the ones you employ directly?"

Glinn looked hard at Wilkinson for a moment.

"I don't see why, Detective."

"Mr Glinn, a man was found dead in his home, badly burnt. Foul play is suspected, and we owe it to him and his family to investigate thoroughly. I'm sure there's nothing in it, but I'd like to have the names in any case, just for the purpose of elimination."

"Very well. Give Monica a call in the office, she'll look after it," Glinn said, handing over a scrap of paper with a number scribbled on it. "Now, can I get on with my work?"

Wilkinson put the note in his pocket and got up, leaving the portacabin and going back to his car, depositing the hard hat with the man at the gate. He sat into his Ford Mondeo, and waited.

As he expected, Glinn appeared a few minutes later and got into his own car – a silver Mercedes saloon parked outside in a pay-and-display bay. Wilkinson could see that Glinn was making a phone call.

While Glinn was still talking, Wilkinson phoned the number that he had been given for Monica. It rang normally, so he knew that Glinn's call was not to his office.

Chapter Twenty-Five

The big red and yellow aircraft taxied slowly across the apron to its usual stand at Dublin Airport. It was a misty night, and the landing lights created an eerie glow around the huge machine as it rolled noisily towards its temporary resting place.

"She's going all the way back to Shanghai direct tonight, so we'd better fill her up good and proper," Joe Donnelly said to his mate, Cathal, as they looked out at the plane that had now stopped and was running down its engines.

"Fair enough," the other man said.

The two of them collected the fuel truck and drove out across the apron to the side of the plane, away from the large cargo door that was now open, revealing the cavernous, brightly lit interior of the freighter.

The crew had departed for their meal break. There were four pilots in all for this rota, and the attendant who would feed and water them on the long journey back east was with them.

Joe and Cathal went through the familiar routine, connecting up the hose and the earthing strap, and started to pump the fuel into the underside of the wing. It would take around forty minutes to complete the operation, and while this was going on, pallets of freight would be unloaded and fresh ones put on board.

At the half hour mark, with all the pallets now dealt with, the familiar security van arrived and ten locked boxes were loaded into the hold normally used for passengers' suitcases, in the belly of the aircraft. Empty boxes were retrieved and placed in the van, which then sped off back into the warren of alleyways and buildings that made up the airport complex.

"Are you OK for a few minutes, Cathal?" Donnelly called out to his mate.

"Yeah, 'course. It'll be another ten minutes before this lot is done."

Donnelly walked around the back of the plane, and keeping close to the fuselage where he was more or less invisible, he approached the aft baggage hold where the boxes had been stowed. He looked around to see if there was anyone observing him. There wasn't. Joe hopped up into the hold and using the keys he had been given, he tried the keys in the locks on the uppermost container. On the fourth attempt, the lock sprang open for him. He quietly eased up the lid and saw rows of black micro-chips neatly placed in their clear plastic sleeves. He slipped a similar looking set out of his inside pocket, and swapped them over before closing the lid and locking it again with the padlock.

He turned around in the confined space, and dropped down silently onto the wet concrete, looking around again to ensure that he had not been seen.

"Are we done yet?" he shouted across to Cathal as he emerged back around to where the fuel bowser was still attached to the wing.

"Just about," Cathal said, climbing up the metal step ladder to detach the nozzle.

Donnelly went to the side of the truck and printed off the delivery docket for the fuel.

"I'll just leave this on the pilot's seat," he said to his mate.

Strictly speaking he should get the docket signed, but if the flight crew weren't there, he often just left the paperwork in the cockpit, and there never seemed to be any issue for the company.

On the way back to the depot, Joe and Cathal met the loadmaster for the freighter and confirmed that it was all fuelled up and ready to go.

"They're still having their dinner inside, but I'll tell them she's ready for off," the man said.

Inside the depot, Joe placed the strip of chips into his holdall, and put it back in his locker, which he secured tightly.

* * *

Wilkinson had persuaded Monica to email him a list of Glinn's employees. He wasn't surprised to find that many of the names were foreign. The construction industry in Ireland relied heavily on Eastern European labour to function. Although a lot of them had departed after the crash of 2008, as building slowly got back to normal levels, a large number of workers had returned to the country where they could earn good money.

Wilkinson contacted a colleague in the Department of Foreign Affairs. He gave her the list and asked her to check out the names to see that they were all properly registered, and in the country legally.

Then he gave a copy of the list to Dónal Lawler and asked him to check the Garda system to see if any of the men had a criminal record, or were known to the force for any reason.

Then he went in search of Burke to bring him up to date.

"Hi, Robert, come in. What's the story?"

Wilkinson filled Burke in on the discussion he had had with the girl at the estate agents and at the building site in Sandymount.

"What do you think? Is there a connection?"

"I'm not sure yet. Glinn was pretty tight-lipped. He claimed he didn't remember anything. But as soon as I left, he went and made a phone call from his car. So, who knows? I'm checking out his employees right now."

"OK. I think it's maybe time I gave the brother a call in the USA." Burke looked at his watch, and said, "It's afternoon in New York now. I'll call him straight away."

Burke looked up the number again and made the call.

"Hello, Mr Phelan. It's Inspector Burke here again from Ireland."

"Oh, right. Have you caught whoever killed my brother yet?"

Burke was a little taken aback by the directness of the man.

"That's not why I'm calling, Mr Phelan. We have received information that there may be some interest in your brother's house. Do you know if he left a will?"

"Nope. I don't know. He never said. Probably not. He wasn't expecting to get shot and burned after all."

"Eh, no, of course not. Anyway, as you seem to be his only next of kin, you might like to talk to a solicitor over here to protect your interest in the property, if indeed it does go to you."

"A solicitor. Is that like an attorney?" Phelan said.

"Yes."

"Look, Inspector, I don't exactly have a lot of spare cash to go paying fancy lawyer fees. What's Tony's place worth anyway? I thought it was just an ex-housing association property."

"Well, I'm not an estate agent, or a 'realtor' as you would say, but it's probably worth in the order of a quarter of a million dollars. But there's something else. Your brother's house was guarding access to a field behind a school which has been re-zoned as residential. If the house was knocked down, the land behind it would be worth a fortune. So, a builder might pay a lot more than the open market value to get hold of Tony's place."

"Wow. Are you serious? I didn't know anything about this."

"Now you see why you need a solicitor – sorry, attorney."

"Yeah, no kidding. How would I go about that?" Phelan said.

"Go on the web. You might be able to get one here in Dublin to act for you on a contingency basis. You know, you pay him a percentage of whatever the yield is from any transaction. But you'll have to sort this out for yourself, Mr Phelan. I'm more interested in catching whoever killed your brother."

"Yeah, I get it. But thanks for the heads up. That's decent of you."

"No problem. Bye."

Chapter Twenty-Six

The following morning, the team assembled for the usual daily catch-up.

"OK, folks. Let's have a look at where we are. By the way, Guy Anderson called me late last night. He'll be joining us in a few minutes. Now, Fiona, what have you got?"

Moore told them about the discussions that they had had with Flanagan from Presswell Exacta the previous day.

"Isn't that a bit dodgy, boss?" Lawler asked.

"Probably. But I don't see any actual laws have been broken here, so I'm happy to let it go, unless of course it leads to any further criminal activity, in which case we'll step in. Better to keep this lot inside the tent in any case, if you ask me."

"Fair enough," Lawler said.

"Robert, what about your investigation into the fire?"

"I contacted Glinn, the builder who had instigated the letter to Tony Phelan, but he wasn't very helpful. I'm getting his workforce checked out now. I should have the information back by lunchtime, or perhaps later on."

"What impression did you get from speaking to him?"

"Slippery, definitely, and cute too."

"Right, stay on it, and let me know when the information on his employees comes through."

"OK, sir."

Just then, Guy Anderson appeared and took a spare seat in the little group.

"Morning, Guy. I hear you had a meet with Joe Donnelly last night. How did it go?" Burke said.

"Hi all. Yes, that's right. He did that little job for me, and he handed over the items from the cargo destined for Shanghai. I'll get them off later on the Delta flight. We have an arrangement with them in place," Anderson said.

"I don't want to know, Guy. Did Donnelly say anything about the camera on board the plane?"

"No, not a word. I don't think he noticed it."

"What's this about a camera?" Moore said.

"The Chinese have put a camera into the hold of the freighter, presumably so they can see if any of the cargo is being tampered with. So, they'll have some nice footage of Joe Donnelly helping himself," Burke said.

"Jesus, boss. Won't that put the man's life in danger?"

"Yes, it will. But I have a plan. When is that China Skies cargo plane due to be in Dublin next?" Burke said.

"I don't know, but I can find out," Moore said.

"Do that, and let me know. If I know anything there will be an extra passenger on board. Someone we'd quite like to talk to."

"Shit! Isn't that a bit risky, boss?" Lawler said.

"Sometimes you have to set a thief to catch a thief, Dónal. Donnelly will be perfectly safe, don't worry."

"If you say so, boss," Lawler said, but wasn't totally convinced.

* * *

As the day wore on, information began to filter back to the detectives. The records for Glinn's employees came through. The foreign workers were clean, with all their paperwork in order, and none had any criminal record – at least none that was recorded on any Irish system.

The Irish employees yielded some more useful information. Glinn had in his employment a man called Malachy O'Neill. He had worked with the builder for five years, but before he took up that employment, he had served a short stretch in Mountjoy Jail for arson. Apparently, a string of lock-up garages at the back of a terrace of houses in Glasnevin had been set on fire, and O'Neill had been caught for it.

Wilkinson brought the news to Moore, who recognised the name of the arresting officer as someone she had worked with in the past.

"Thanks, Robert. I know Jimmy Mulvihill. I worked with him for a while when I was on secondment to Drumcondra. I'll give them a call and see if he's still there."

Moore got through to Mulvihill almost immediately.

"Oh, hi, Fiona. Long time no see. How the hell are ya?"

"Hi, Jimmy. Ah, you know. So-so. Anyway, I'm calling about an arrest you made a few years back, of a Malachy O'Neill. You did him for arson. Something about a few garages at the back of some houses. Do you remember?"

"God, yes, I certainly do. A right little toe rag that one. He's been pretty active with his petrol can and matches for a while, but we could never get enough evidence to nail him. But eventually, we got lucky. He fell through the roof of a place he had set fire to and broke his leg. The firemen got him out just before the whole lot went up, and he was banged to rights. And when we nabbed him, he fessed up to the Glasnevin job – but it was just one of a number of places he had torched," Mulvihill said.

"What was his game?" Moore said.

"Who knows. I think he just liked playing with matches. Has he turned up on your patch?"

"Possibly. It's a long story, but he may be involved. What was his MO?"

"Simple stuff. A can of petrol and a box of matches. He'd set the fire and then take off. That was why he was so hard to catch. Usually these guys hang around to observe their handiwork, but not our Malachy. And he always had a good alibi too. So, it was a bit of a blessing when he fell through the roof."

"OK, thanks a million, Jimmy. I think we'll be having a word with Malachy."

"Nice. Well, give him my regards. And, hey, don't be a stranger!"

"OK. Thanks, Jimmy. Talk soon."

When Moore had finished the call, Wilkinson said, "Shall I bring him in?"

"No, not yet anyway. I'd like to do a bit more investigating on Glinn. Have a root around. See if he's been involved in any other properties that went on fire mysteriously."

"OK. I'll see what I can find out."

* * *

By mid-afternoon, the team had received a lot of information, and they got back together to share it out before going home for the night.

Moore started with her news. She relayed the information she had received on Malachy O'Neill. Burke agreed that it would be premature to bring him in, and stressed that they needed some evidence to link him to the fire at Tony Phelan's house, if they weren't going to look foolish. Burke was certain that Glinn would have another sleazy lawyer to get O'Neill off the hook unless they had a watertight case.

Moore had also had word back from the airport about the next arrival of the China Skies freighter. It would be back in the following night at around ten o'clock.

"Excellent. When we have finished here, I'll get onto the airport and set things up. I want us all to convene here at six o'clock tomorrow afternoon, and don't make any plans for the rest of the evening."

"Care to share?" Lawler said.

"All in good time, Dónal, all in good time."

Guy Anderson was the next to speak.

"Does your plan include me, Inspector?"

"I don't think so, Guy. If it all goes pear-shaped, I don't want you caught up in the mess. When are you going back to the USA anyway?" Burke said.

"Well, I'm nearly done here. I've got all I came for. We have a good connection with Presswell Exacta now, thanks to your efforts, and I have the samples that we need for further analysis, so there's not really anything to detain me. But if it's OK with you, I'd like to stay on for a day or two just to see if your guys can round this out. I've got a bit attached to the whole thing."

"Fine by me. But I'll have to ask you to stay in the background, Guy."

"No problem. You won't even know I'm here."

"OK, then. If we're all done, I better go and brief the Super. See you all in the morning."

Chapter Twenty-Seven

"Hi, Janet. Look, I know this is ridiculously short notice, and you've probably got plans, but is there any chance you'd be free for dinner this evening? I could pick you up at seven-thirty or eight?" Wilkinson said when he got through to McBrien's office.

"Hmm... let me see," she said as she feigned looking through her long list of social engagements.

"I suppose I could move a few things around, if you're desperate, but it depends on where you're planning to take me," she said.

"How about a surprise?" Wilkinson said.

"How about Tomahawk in Temple Bar? A person gets hungry doing nothing all day."

Tomahawk was a fabulous steakhouse located in Dublin's left bank area, and was known for its enormous and succulent beef.

"OK, you're on. Text me your address and I'll see you at 7:45. OK?"

"Will you be bringing your handcuffs?" she said, laughing.

"Cheeky!" He hung up.

His phone pinged a few moments later with Janet's address in Ballsbridge, and a couple of yellow smiley faces.

* * *

Moore decided that she wouldn't go directly home that evening. She drove out along Amiens Street, where the rush hour traffic was almost at a standstill. Feeling impatient, she put on the blue lights in her car, and nipped up along the bus lane, all the way up to Annesley Bridge. The traffic had eased out a bit there, so she turned off the lights and continued on up through Fairview to Tony Phelan's burnt-out shell of a house.

As she parked the car and got out, she was trying to piece together the events that had led to the man's killing, and the fire. The pathologist had told them that Tony Phelan was dead before he was cremated, although both events had taken place on the same night.

Moore walked up the lane at the side of the house, and in through the metal gate onto the school grounds.

"OK, so our Chinese killer gets over the back fence, approaches the house and sees Tony in the kitchen, sneaks up to the back door and fires through the glass, hitting Tony in the back. Happy that he has achieved his objective, he retreats back the way he came, losing his weapon in the long grass, and makes off," she said to herself.

"Sometime later, the arsonist with his can of petrol arrives, and uses the same approach to the house. He sees the broken back window, and decides to pour the accelerant in through it onto the kitchen floor, and set the whole lot alight. He mustn't have seen the body of Tony lying on the floor – why would he? After all, it was probably pitch dark by then."

Moore retraced the steps the arsonist would have taken, and noticed that the amount of glass removed from the rear door of the house was considerably more than would be left by a single shot. She took out her torch and closely examined the back door.

"I wonder if our friend had to remove some glass in order to insert the nozzle of his jerry-can, or whatever receptacle he was using. The fireman said that there was no spillage outside the house, so he must have pushed it well in to pour it on the floor," she mused to herself.

She went back to her car and called a contact in the forensic team and asked them to come back to the house to carry out a very detailed examination of the back door, and to look in particular for skin flakes or a small quantity of blood on the glass. She figured the arsonist would have had to remove his gloves – assuming he was wearing them in the first place – in order to take out the bits of glass and deposit the petrol in through the back door.

As she waited outside for the forensic team to arrive, the woman from the next-door house came out.

"Oh, it's you, Sergeant. I was wondering who was snooping about in poor Tony's garden," Elsie O'Brien said. "Have you caught the bugger that did this yet?"

"Not yet, Mrs O'Brien, but we have a definite line of enquiry we are following."

Moore could tell by the woman's dismissive demeanour that she wasn't impressed, assuming it to be just a standard line that the Gardaí put out when they hadn't a clue what was going on.

"What has you back here, anyway?" Mrs O'Brien went on.

"I'm just waiting for some of our technical folks to arrive out. We have a bit more work to do at the back of the house."

"Ah, right. I'll leave you at it, so," she said, turning her back on Moore and shuffling back up the path into her own house.

Twenty minutes later, the white 4x4 with the yellow stripe along its side pulled in behind Moore's car. She got out and greeted the forensic officer whom she knew from several previous encounters.

"Hi, Phil. Thanks for coming out," she said.

"Hi, Fiona. What's the story here?"

"I'd like you to do a very careful examination of the back door. The glass, the frame and all around. And while you're at it, have a look down the drains at the back too. I don't think that was done first time around."

"Lovely! What are we looking for?" Phil said.

"It's already been gone over, but that was in the heat of the moment, if you'll excuse the pun. I'm hoping we might be able to get some traces of DNA left behind by the arsonist. I think he may have taken his gloves off to pour in the accelerant, and with all that broken glass, he may have left something. Anyway, I know you'll find it if there's anything there."

"OK. I'll get Aoife all suited up, and we'll do it together. Are you going to hang around?"

"Yep, may as well. I've nothing else on anyway. I'll wait in the car."

The two forensic officers donned white paper suits and took a pair of very bright LED lamps with them, along with a variety of tools of their trade, as they made their way to the rear of Tony Phelan's house.

Moore sat into her car and turned on the radio. She tuned it in to Sunshine 106 where they were playing a medley of old tunes from the 1970s and 1980s. She reclined the driver's seat a little, and after a few minutes dozed off.

Phil woke her with a start by tapping on the window, and she sat bolt upright, taking a second or two to re-orient herself. Then she pressed her finger on the button and wound down the driver's window.

"Sorry, Phil. I must have dropped off for a moment. Have you finished?"

"Yes, we have. I'm taking some of the glass back to the lab. I think you're right. There may be some tiny traces of something. It could be paint, but maybe not. Anyway, we'll know in the morning. Oh, and we found a shell case in the waste in the back yard. Right down at the bottom of the drain, stuck in all that lovely sludge. It's quite small. Looks about right for the 7.62 calibre weapon. I'll have it checked out in the morning. Is there anything else you need this evening?"

"No, that's all. Thanks a lot. What time is it anyway?"

"Just after seven. OK, we'll pack up and go. I'll call you in the morning."

Chapter Twenty-Eight

Robert Wilkinson pulled his Audi into the car park in front of Janet's apartment block off Sandymount Avenue at the side of the old AIB complex. The building was on three floors in total, with two apartments to either side of the front door, making twelve units in all. By the look of the place, it had been built in the 1970s. It had a brick front, and a concrete awning suspended over the main entrance which featured twin glazed doors in teak. At the left of the door, a stack of doorbells was fastened into the wall.

Wilkinson approached and found the bell with a small piece of white paper bearing the name 'J Fallon' in pale blue ink. He pressed the bell, and after a moment Janet's voice came through.

"Yes," she said.

"Hi, it's Rob."

"Oh, hi. You're very punctual. C'mon up."

A buzzer sounded and the twin glass doors were released. Wilkinson entered, noting the smell of polish coming from the vinyl tiles on the floor and climbed the stairs to the first floor. Apartment six was on the left of the stairwell and the door to Janet's place stood ajar.

Wilkinson pushed the door open and went in. Janet was inside in the spacious and tastefully furnished sitting room, just tidying her hair in the mirror over the fireplace. When she turned around, Wilkinson could see that she had made a lot of effort to look good.

"Wow, you look amazing!" Wilkinson said, walking over to her. She was dressed in very well-cut blue denim jeans that accentuated her trim figure, topped by a dusty pink woollen polo neck jumper, again very well fitting. Her brown leather jacket completed the ensemble.

Janet presented her cheek and Rob kissed it briefly. Then she stood back, and flicked her shoulder-length blonde hair with her hand, saying, "Well, a girl has to do her best. OK, shall we go?"

Downstairs, Wilkinson went to the passenger's door of his car, holding it open and closing it when the Janet was comfortably inside.

"So, did you manage to get a table for us at Tomahawk?" Janet asked as they turned right at the top of Sandymount Avenue and drove towards town, past the regal façade of the Royal Dublin Society.

"Yep! No problem."

"God, you're gas. That place is booked up for weeks ahead. How did you swing it?"

"If I told you that, I'd have to kill you! No, you'd be surprised how working for the fraud squad can open doors."

"Fraud squad? You didn't tell me that."

"You didn't ask. Anyway, remember, no shop talk."

"Ah, OK."

"So, how long have you lived in that apartment?" Wilkinson said.

"I've been there since I started with McBriens. It's only rented, but Frank got it for me. He has some arrangement with a number of landlords – something to do with maintenance and repairs. The owner lives abroad, so I get it at a reduced rent if we agree to keep it in good condition, but to be honest, it doesn't ask for much."

"That's handy."

"Perk of the job – like getting a table at short notice in a fully booked restaurant!" Janet said.

"Fair enough. Point taken."

* * *

Wilkinson continued with the chivalry at the restaurant. He pulled Janet's chair out for her to take her seat, and moved it in as she sat down. They studied the menu in silence for a few minutes, and then Janet said, "Would you go the T-bone with me?"

Tomahawk specialized in a 20-ounce T-bone steak for two which was always cooked to perfection and was melt-in-the-mouth delicious.

"Sure – go for it!" he said, closing the menu. "And what wine would you like?"

"You choose."

They ordered their meal and sat back.

"So, tell me about Janet, Janet."

"What would you like to know?"

"Oh, I dunno. Like, have you any brothers and sisters? Hobbies? Secret lovers? That sort of thing."

"Jesus! You're not really direct, are you. I have one sister – two years younger before you ask – Caroline."

"And is she blonde and beautiful like her big sister?" Wilkinson said.

"No, she's not. She has almost black hair, like our mother. Dad isn't fair either. They don't know where I got my colouring from – Dad says he thinks I must be the milkman's."

"Ha. What does your mother say?"

"She's saying nothing! And as for secret lovers, you must be joking."

"OK, but you must have quite a few admirers, I mean, look at you, you're gorgeous."

"And I'm very, very fussy. Mum says I'll end up a miserable old hag if I don't compromise. Nobody's perfect etcetera, etcetera. But I dunno, no sign of Mr Right just yet anyway."

"Plenty of time. What about hobbies?"

"Don't laugh. Flying."

"Flying? Flying what?"

"Light aircraft. I'm training for my Private Pilot's Licence. I just love it. The freedom. The open skies – woman and machine in harmony. Ever done any?"

"Nope, never, but I can see the attraction. Where do you fly from?"

"Weston mostly. But I've flown in and out of Dublin Airport once or twice too. If you're not careful, I'll take you up one day," Janet said.

"OK. If you're not careful, I might accept!"

Just then their meal arrived, and they turned their attention to the food.

The meal was magnificent, and Wilkinson was surprised at the ease with which Janet demolished her share. They had no room for dessert, and when the waiter asked them if they would like some coffee, Janet said, "Why don't we do that at my place?"

Wilkinson paid the bill and left a good tip. He was feeling generous.

Back at her apartment, as she made them both coffee from a very posh machine, Wilkinson turned the conversation to McBrien and his enterprise.

"How does McBrien make his money then? Those properties I saw in the window of the shop would hardly be enough to keep the place open."

"You're right. He has other interests. Him and that guy Glinn do a lot together."

"What sort of things?"

"I shouldn't really tell you this, but what the hell. Frank identifies listed properties that have fallen into disrepair and picks them up for a song. Nobody is really interested in them, because they cost a fortune to restore with all the regulations and conditions, and even then, they are rarely viable units. A few of them have burnt down, and then of course they can be demolished without any concerns about the listing. Glinn makes a packet out of it, and I presume he splits the proceeds with Frank."

"Wow. Have you shared this information with anyone?"

"None of my concern. I just mind my own business and get on with my work. And besides, it could be risky to get involved with those types. The job suits me, so I don't want to rock the boat. Anyway, who would I tell?"

"Yeah, I see what you mean. And you could put yourself in danger."

"You won't do anything about what I've said, Rob, will you?"

"If I do, I won't involve you, that's for sure, but it might be time to start looking for another job."

"Terrific," Janet said, rolling her eyes to heaven.

Chapter Twenty-Nine

The following day was busy. There was a lot to organise, and much of it was based on a hunch that Burke had; so, if the wheels came off, he would look like a right eejit. Furthermore, Superintendent Jerome Heffernan would be furious about the waste of money, but it was a chance Burke felt he had to take.

Before getting stuck into the arrangements, Burke called Moore into his office.

"Do you think we're doing the right thing, Fiona?"

"I'll tell you tomorrow."

"No, seriously, what do you think?"

"It's the same old story, boss. If it comes off, you'll be a hero. If it doesn't, you could end up back in uniform. Me too, by the way."

"I hear you. But I dunno, I have a feeling in my water about this. I think we should go ahead," Burke said.

"Yeah, I think you're right. But let's make sure we keep Donnelly well away from the action. You never know what he'd get up to. He's a bloody hot head. I'd better get on and make the arrangements. If I need to pull rank, I'll get back to you."

"OK. Chat later."

Moore went back to her desk and called the Chief Airport Police Officer and told him the plan. She requested unmarked cars to be placed close to all of the gates that lead out of the airport complex, particularly the ones used by the construction workers over on the south side of the airfield.

"Do they need to be armed?" the man asked.

"That's up to you, sir. But we expect our target to have a weapon of some kind. He's used a gun before."

"Right. We'll draw arms, so."

Next, she called the Chief Operating Officer for the Airport Authority. The woman wasn't available, but called her back fifteen minutes later.

"Hello, Sergeant, this is Marie Keogh from the airport, you were looking for me."

"Hello, Ms Keogh, yes, thanks for calling back. I was wondering how we might set up something for tonight out at the airport. We need a plane parked close to where the China Skies aircraft docks when it comes in from Shanghai. Can that be arranged?"

"Hold on. Let me see. We usually park the China Skies on stand one-o-two. It's convenient for the loading and unloading of the freight, and they also have a special delivery on most trips, so it's handy if it's always in the same place. What's going on anyway?"

"We have an operation out there tonight. Your Chief of Police is in the picture. Do you think you could get an aircraft parked up on an adjacent stand? On the same side as the cargo door of the freighter, and just leave it open with steps up front and back?"

"Well, I'll have to check with the airlines, but I imagine we could do that for you. Will there be any risk to the aircraft?"

"No, nothing like that. We just need somewhere to keep a few officers out of sight when the China Skies plane comes in. And could you make sure that the doors to the baggage holds are left open? Our people will stay in there till they are needed."

"Yes, OK. Let me see what I can arrange. Is it OK if I call you back a bit later?"

"Yes, that would be fine. And thanks for your help."

Next, Moore called Davern at Jet59.

"Hello, Mr Davern, it's Sergeant Moore here from Store Street. I was wondering if you could tell me if Joe Donnelly is working tonight, please?"

"Hold on a moment, Sergeant, I'll check the roster. Why do you want to know anyway?"

"I'll tell you in a minute. Is he on tonight?"

"Let's see. Yes, he is. Cathal and him are on from eight to two. What's going on?"

"We'll be doing some work out there later on. We'd like to put one of our men on the truck that fuels the China Skies plane. And we'd like Joe Donnelly to stay in the depot. Can you fix that for us?"

"I suppose so, but what's all this about?"

"The less you know, the better. One of our guys will come out to you at eight o'clock and you can get someone to show him the ropes. Can you stay on to meet him and make the introductions?"

"Yes, I suppose so. Get him to come to the office and I'll sort it out. But I wish you'd tell me what's going on. Are any of my men in danger?"

"Thanks for your help, Mr Davern, we'll be in touch."

* * *

As luck would have it, it was a foggy night in Dublin when the Gardaí assembled in the Airport Police building for a briefing.

"Do you think it will lift?" Burke said to the Airport Police Chief.

"Na, it's down for the night. But there's still traffic coming and going. You'll probably be OK."

"I hope so. OK, let's get set up."

Burke had collected up a number of Gardaí from the night shift at Store Street, and six additional men from the Armed Response Unit. He divided the men up into teams of three, the third person in each case being an Airport Police Officer, as they knew the geography of the place well.

Moore and Lawler were to be positioned in the spare plane that had been parked on stand one-o-four, as requested, with all its doors open and steps up to the front and rear entrances. The baggage hold doors in the belly of the aircraft had also been left open, and a buggy with two empty luggage trailers had been left alongside for authenticity.

Wilkinson had been teamed up with the fuelling crew, and was being shown how to attach the earthing strap to the side of the aircraft when it came to rest, and roll out the hose. His companion, Cathal, would actually attach the device to the plane, leaving Wilkinson free to handle whatever cropped up. Unlike Moore and Lawler, Wilkinson had not drawn a firearm, as he wasn't trained to use a gun.

There was a palpable tension in the room as the briefing continued.

"Where is the plane now?" Burke said.

"About one hour and forty minutes out according to Flightradar. He's at 37,000 feet and doing 390 knots. ETA 10:04."

"OK. Let's get in position by 9:00 and do a radio check. Are all your guys ready to rock and roll, Chief?"

"Yes, they are, with instructions to stop and apprehend anyone coming out of any of the gates or over the fence. They all have radios too."

"Great. Any questions, anyone?"

No one spoke.

Chapter Thirty

"China Skies seven-zero-six, Dublin," the pilot said into his microphone.

"China seven-zero-six, identified on handover, re-cleared to seven thousand feet, and maintain the heading two-nine-zero. Weather is Papa."

"Roger, Dublin. Seven thousand and maintain heading two-nine-zero. China Skies seven-zero-six."

The pilot tuned his secondary radio to the Dublin VOLMET frequency and noted the automated readout. He was concerned to find that visibility was down to less than two kilometres and there was fog right down to ground level, with no significant change forecast.

"China Skies seven-zero-six, Dublin. Can you confirm that the field is still open? What's the visibility like?"

"China, yes, we're still operational. The fog is coming and going. You should be able to get in OK, but if not, be prepared for a diversion to Shannon."

The pilot clicked the transmit button twice, indicating that he had received the information.

A few minutes later, the voice of the Dublin controller crackled in his earpiece again.

"China Skies seven-zero-six, cleared ILS approach runway two-eight, and confirm when you have the runway in sight."

"Roger, cleared ILS for two-eight, report runway in sight."

The pilot watched the cross hairs on the instrument in front of him as the huge machine turned slightly onto the runway heading. He was a little high on the glideslope, so he eased the throttle back a fraction till the plane was perfectly positioned for the runway.

The plane descended till it was at two hundred and fifty feet, and still there was no sign of the bright lights that would tell the pilot there was a runway ahead.

"China Skies seven-zero-six going around," he called to the tower.

"Roger, China, straight ahead to 3,000 feet and then a right turn onto 010 for further instructions. Maintain 3,000 on reaching."

The pilot squeezed the TOGA buttons on the sides of the thrust levers and the giant engines spooled up to a crescendo as the nose of the plane lifted away from the ground. The co-pilot raised the undercarriage and partially retracted the flaps, and the aircraft climbed quickly to the designated altitude.

On the ground, the Gardaí heard the screaming of the engines but could see nothing.

"China seven-zero-six, do you want to try from the other end?"

"Yes, please. Can you give us the vectors?"

"Maintain 3,000 feet and execute a procedural turn to your left to capture the zero-one-zero ILS, then descend as per the instruments. I think you'll get in this time, it appears to be lifting a little."

"Roger, Dublin. Left turn to capture the zero-one-zero ILS. Maintaining 3,000 feet. Will advise when established."

The pilot brought the Airbus around as instructed and captured the cross hairs on his instrument that would guide him to the reciprocal end of Dublin's main runway.

"China skies seven-zero-six fully established ILS for zero-one-zero."

"Roger, China, cleared to land runway zero-one-zero, wind calm."

As the aircraft descended towards the ground, at 350 feet the pilot could see the two strips of bright landing lights just beginning to appear through the mist.

"China seven-zero-six, runway in sight."

"Roger, China, continue."

And with a large puff of blue smoke from the tires, the machine touched down at 10:22 p.m. and slowed to taxiing speed.

"China Skies on at 10:22. Take the next convenient left, then contact ground one-two-one decimal eight. Good night."

"One-two-one eight. Thanks."

The pilot was instructed to follow the usual route along the taxiways and park on the normal stand, one-o-two.

Moore and Lawler were dressed in high-viz jackets and had woolly hats and ear defenders on as they tried to make themselves look busy working on the spare plane that had been parked close to where the China Skies aircraft would stop.

They saw the huge machine approaching though the mist, the bright lights on the nose wheel struts creating a massive halo effect as it slowly edged towards them. Even with the ear defenders, the noise of its two enormous turbo-fans was deafening, and they were relieved when it finally came to rest and they were shut down.

"China Skies is parked now. Stand by," Moore said into her radio, the microphone of which had been clipped to the inside of her lapel.

As the whine of the engines faded away, the front door of the A300 opened, and the single flight attendant guided the steps into position with hand signals to the driver. Then he disappeared back inside the plane, and a moment later the huge cargo door in the left-hand forward fuselage began to open, revealing the cargo inside.

Moore saw the flight crew leaving by the forward steps. There were four of them in all, and they were followed up by the flight attendant. A minibus had drawn up close to the foot of the steps, and the five of them got in. It then set off through the mist for the terminal where no doubt the crew would be fed and watered.

The large mechanical handling machines were positioned underneath the cargo door, and after a few minutes, the first pallet was rolled out onto the elevated section and lowered slowly to the ground, where it was pushed onto a low trailer.

Three more pallets were off-loaded in the same manner, and then there was a short delay as the low loader was driven away and replaced by another empty one. Unloading resumed. Moore was watching the operation carefully. As the next pallet started its journey out of the plane, she spotted the figure of a man dressed in black, clinging to the back of the pallet using its straps to support him.

"Suspect leaving the plane now. We're closing in," she said into her radio as she grabbed Lawler by the arm and started walking towards the China Skies aircraft.

Li Jun saw the two of them approaching, and jumped down from the plane when the load was just three feet off the ground. He sprinted towards the buggy hitched to the front of the two baggage trolleys that had been left out to feign authenticity beside the second aeroplane, and jumped in.

Moore and Lawler gave chase, but before they could catch him, he had powered up the buggy and driven off at speed into the mist.

"Shit!" Moore exclaimed.

"Suspect on the move. He's taken a baggage cart and is heading south across the apron. We're following on foot," she said rather breathlessly into her radio as the two of them set off in pursuit.

Li Jun had a rough idea of the airport layout from his previous visit. He knew there was a gate used by construction workers that was rarely closed on the southern perimeter, and he pointed the vehicle in that direction.

As he drove across the apron as quickly as the baggage truck would permit, he narrowly missed the front of a taxiing Aer Lingus A330 that was heading for its appointed gate. The pilot saw the baggage truck just in time, and stood on the brakes, stopping the nosewheel just a couple of metres short of the fleeing buggy.

Lawler and Moore were losing their quarry. It was just a little too quick for them, and helped by the misty conditions, they were running out of breath. Moore pulled up and gasped into her radio once more, "Suspect is escaping. He's still heading south towards the perimeter fence. Someone go after him before we lose him altogether!"

"Fuck this. I've had enough of the little shit," Joe Donnelly said, leaping to the door of the Jet59 hut before Burke could stop him. Outside, Donnelly jumped into the old van that was kept there for carrying engine oil and other parts around the airport, started it, and drove out of the yard with wheels spinning. Donnelly knew the layout of the airport apron very well, and he easily found a disused taxiway that would take him across to the southern boundary quickly. As he drove along, pushing the old van as hard as he could, he spotted Li Jun careering in much the same direction, at an angle to his own trajectory.

Donnelly floored the old van, and struck the buggy midships, turning it over in a cacophony of tearing metal and smoke. Both vehicles came to rest. Joe Donnelly had hurt himself quite badly in the crash, but Li Jun had reacted more quickly, and jumped clear just before impact, and now set off running, using the fog for cover.

Donnelly shook himself out of semi-consciousness and grabbed the radio.

"He's headed for gate 21 on foot. For Christ sake, would someone stop the man before he gets away."

The two Airport Police officers that were sitting in their car outside gate 21 heard the message on their radio. They got out of their vehicle hurriedly, and went to the gate, positioning themselves one on each side of the exit, and crouched down. Moments later, they saw the shadowy figure of Li Jun emerging from the mist and hobbling in their direction. As he passed through the gap, they sprang at him from both sides and wrestled him to the ground, causing him to drop the holdall which he had miraculously managed to keep with him till that point. A few seconds later, they had him in handcuffs, and had dragged him towards their car, opened the rear doors and put him inside.

"Suspect apprehended at gate 21. He's cuffed, and in the back of the car," the female police officer said into the radio.

Within a further three minutes, several more vehicles had arrived at the gate, one of which contained Inspector Aidan Burke. As they gathered around the car holding their captive, Moore and Lawler arrived on foot, totally out of breath and looking bedraggled after their exertions.

"We have him," Burke said to his two colleagues.

Chapter Thirty-One

"That was an excellent night's work, folks. Thank you all for your effort. Now, we need to get on with things this morning to tidy it all up. Is Donnelly OK?" Burke asked.

"Yeah, he's fine. He was a bit woozy after his Lewis Hamilton impersonation, but they patched him up at the depot and he went into St James's for a check-up just in case."

"Excellent. Now, what was in yer man's holdall?"

"Interesting. Amongst a few bits and pieces – you know, toothbrush, a clean pair of socks – there was a dagger. Nasty looking thing. I've had a quick look on the web, and it seems to be a Loong Dagger. Forensics have it now to see if they can get any dabs or DNA off it."

"Lovely. I wonder who was going to benefit from an encounter with that!" Burke said.

"My guess is Donnelly. They must have filmed him lifting the micro-chips from the container and sent Li Jun over to deal with him," Moore said.

"Speaking of which, how is our overseas visitor?"

"We had great fun last night. He's pretending he doesn't speak English, so we had to get an interpreter on the phone in order to book him in. But I imagine he's putting it on," Lawler said.

"Terrific. Have we someone lined up for the interview?" Burke said.

"Yes. We have an interpreter coming in at ten, along with a duty solicitor," Lawler said.

"What about the air crew?"

"They've gone back. They denied all knowledge of the man. Said he was a stowaway. Your friend the Chief of the Airport Police took statements and made them fill out about a hundred forms – you know, indemnity, waving their rights, and lots of other stuff, then he let them go at about 3:00 a.m.," Moore said.

"Hmph... stowaway my arse! Still, hard to prove anything different, I suppose. OK, will you and Dónal do the interview with the guy? I'd better go upstairs and brief Heffernan. And let me know if forensics can tie anything to the gun we found in Phelan's garden."

"Right, boss. Chat later," Moore said.

* * *

"Come in, Aidan, take a seat," Superintendent Jerome Heffernan said as Burke entered his office.

"Morning, sir. I just thought I'd better bring you up to date with the Tony Phelan case, and all the other stuff that's being going on with your American friend."

Burke proceeded to tell his senior officer about the capture of Li Jun out at the airport, and their efforts to link the man to the murder of Tony Phelan. He gave a brief account of the business with the micro-chips too, but noticed Heffernan glazing over as soon as it got in any way technical.

"So, where's our American friend now, then?" Heffernan said.

"He'll be heading home today or tomorrow. He's got what he came for. They are going to implant a guy in

Presswell Exacta – with the full co-operation of the owner of course."

"I'm glad I'm not in that business, Aidan. You never know what's going on or who to trust."

Just then, Heffernan's phone rang.

He signalled Burke to wait while he took the call. Heffernan gave nothing away during the call which lasted all of five minutes. Just the occasional "I see" and "Yes, of course" was all that was said from his end.

When the call was over, he looked Burke straight in the eye.

"That was Stephen Green – the Permanent Undersecretary to the Minister for Foreign Affairs, no less. Seems we've hit a nerve, again, or rather you have."

"Oh, oh. Let me guess, Li Jun?"

"I can see why we made you a detective, Aidan. Got it in one."

"What about him?"

"Yer man was on about how much trade we have with China and how valuable it is to our economy. How this incident could cause severe embarrassment to the government. Possible loss of jobs – yada yada yada."

"What did he want you to do?" Burke said.

"Oh, no, they're much subtler than that. 'I know you'll do the right thing, Superintendent' was what I got. Bullshit!"

"Yeah, but hold on a sec. This guy has murdered one of our citizens in cold blood, and would have done another if we hadn't caught him. We can't just let that go, can we?"

"No, Aidan, we can't. But neither can we haul the guy up in front of the courts. All this crap about Presswell would have to come out and God knows what the consequences would be. No, we won't be taking him to court. Not this time."

"What then?"

"Well, now, Aidan. You're a man of the world. I'm sure you can figure something out, but for God's sake, keep me out of it."

"Great! So, you want me to clean up this mess for you, sir, is that it?"

"That's what we pay you for, Aidan."

Burke said no more in case he would say too much. He got up and left the office, resisting the temptation to slam the door behind him.

* * *

When Burke got back downstairs to his office, Guy Anderson was waiting to see him.

"I just thought I'd stop by to say farewell and thank you for your help, Inspector."

"Oh, OK, you're off then?"

"Yep! I'm all done here, for now in any case."

"You know, I was thinking about your plan to embed a techy in Presswell. Do you not think that the Chinese will find out when he starts making changes to the chips?"

Anderson looked Burke in the eye for quite a while.

"Probably," he said eventually.

"And then they'll almost certainly stop using Presswell altogether, won't they?"

"Probably."

"And when that happens, Flanagan's business will be more or less stuffed, unless you have gotten him a lot more contracts from Singapore or wherever."

Anderson just continued to look impassively at Burke.

"God, you bastard. There aren't any new contracts, are there? You want the Chinese to find out and effectively close Flanagan down, don't you?"

"All's fair in love and war, Aidan," Anderson said, shrugging his shoulders.

"Not so fast. That man has a good business. He employs highly skilled operatives that all pay taxes. He'll be ruined."

"Don't be naïve, Aidan. The guy's a crook. He's bringing in cocaine from China in case you didn't remember. And anyway, he'll start up again in a year or two and make piles of dough doing something else."

"Why not work with our people in the drug squad and bring him to book? With the information you have on him, and the evidence from the factory we found, it would be a slam dunk, as you folks say."

"Jesus, Aidan, give me a break. That's not the way we work, and you should be thankful for it. Your government don't want this whole thing blasted all across the world in the media. Look at the reputational damage that it would do to little old Ireland. Not to mention the impact on your Chinese students' attendance here. They pay three times what an EU citizen pays to places like Trinity College and UCD. No, much better to do it quietly and unobtrusively. That way, there's no knock-on effect."

"Damn it, Guy, I'm not up to all this subterfuge and spy shit. I'm just an ordinary copper doing my best with some pretty nasty people doing bad things in my town. I presume you have authority for all this covert carry-on?"

"You better believe it. From the highest level – and I mean the highest."

"Who the hell are you, Guy?"

The American laughed.

"Why, I'm just an American tourist here to see the Book of Kells, Aidan."

"Yeah, right, and I'm bloody Lieutenant Columbo!"

"Look, Aidan, don't go all prissy on me. You're a damn fine cop. And your team have impressed me a whole lot too. That Fiona Moore is top notch. She's gonna go far, trust me. Let's just shake hands as friends, eh?"

"Hmm... OK, you're right, Guy. Anyway, I have some diplomatic stunts to set up myself. Look, thanks for your help, and maybe we'll meet again some time."

"I don't doubt it, Aidan."

Guy Anderson got up and left the station.

Chapter Thirty-Two

Fiona Moore and Dónal Lawler had interviewed Li Jun for almost four hours. It was a tortuous process, what with the interpreter and the constant interruptions from Jun's Irish solicitor telling them they couldn't ask this and that, and that they couldn't accuse him of anything without concrete evidence.

Halfway through the morning, Moore began to realise that the whole thing was a charade in any case. None of it felt right.

Even when their progress was punctuated by the forensic report which showed that a partial fingerprint recovered from the shell cartridge was a seventy percent match to a print taken from the man himself.

"Do you really think you'll get a conviction based on that?" the man laughed at them.

By lunch time, Moore had had enough. She suspended proceedings and went in search of Burke to tell him the bad news.

"It's fucking hopeless, boss. I thought we might be able to frighten him into making a confession, but no chance. Would you like to have a go?" Moore said.

"Nope! Thanks all the same. Let's go to plan B."

"Plan B?"

"Yes. See if you can find Joe Donnelly. I want to speak to him. You do too, by the way."

"I do? OK. What's going on?"

"You'll see. Just find out where he is and come and tell me. OK?"

"OK."

Moore was back a few minutes later.

"Donnelly's out at the airport. He's on earlies this week. He's there till two-thirty."

Burke looked at his watch.

"Great. Let's go."

Moore could get no more information from Burke on the drive out to the airport. They swung in through the gates of the Jet59 yard, and spotted Joe Donnelly coming out of one of the buildings getting ready to go home.

Burke stopped the car. The two detectives got out and approached Donnelly.

"Hi, Joe. Glad to see there's no lasting damage. Can we have a word?"

"I'm just clocking off. Why don't we go down to the pub? I need to get some lunch anyway."

"Is that The Boot Inn?"

"Yeah. You can follow me if you like. It's only a couple of minutes away."

Donnelly got into his car and drove out of the yard and round in front of a vast hangar where a Boeing 747 was being pulled apart for a D check. They arrived at a side entrance to the complex, and a man in a high-viz jacket saluted Joe and let them out onto the back road. A moment later they were at the pub.

When they had ordered some food, Donnelly said, "What's on your minds?"

Burke outlined his plan to the man.

"Once we deliver him to you, Joe, it's up to you how you handle it. We're not too bothered about what happens to him, but I don't want any dead bodies showing up on my turf. Got it?"

"I understand, Inspector. Don't worry, me and the lads will take care of things."

"Good man, Joe, I knew we could rely on you. I'll have him out to you about nine o'clock tonight. OK?"

"Yes, fine. Don't bring him inside. I'll hang around just outside our compound in my own car, and you can hand him over there."

"Fine. See you later then."

Burke and Moore left the pub and drove back towards town.

"What's happening, Aidan? This sounds very dodgy to me."

Burke explained the conversations he had had with both Superintendent Heffernan and Guy Anderson earlier in the day.

"It seems we need to send a message back to China. They have already sent us one, after all. And it all has to be done with smoke and mirrors – nothing overt – nothing that could cause waves diplomatically."

"I see. And are you sure we won't get hung out to dry, boss?" Moore said.

"As certain as I can be with all these bloody coded messages. You'll be OK, anyway. If the shit hits the fan, I'll be in the firing line."

"Won't Heffernan provide cover?"

"I doubt it if it gets really tricky. But I don't think it will. I think we'll be fine. By the way, what's Wilkinson doing?" Burke said.

"I have him following up on the fire, and whatever is going on with McBrien and Glinn."

"Good. That's more in his line anyway."

* * *

Joe Donnelly didn't go home. He went back to the airport and sought out a mate of his who worked as an electrician on aircraft.

He found him in the hangar getting ready to do some work on an A320 that had some minor problem.

"Hiya, Dom. Have you got a minute?"

"Oh. Hi, Joe. Sure. What has you over here in these parts?"

"I just need to find out something about the electrics on those A300s – you know the ones that the China crowd use for freight."

"OK," Dominic said, looking curiously at Joe, "no bother, I have the diagrams for that ship over here by the desk."

Dominic spent half an hour explaining how the circuits that Joe was interested in worked, and how to access the control panel in the cockpit of the giant aircraft to affect their behaviour.

Joe noted down a few things on a scrap of paper and tucked it into his inside pocket. When he had all he needed, he bade farewell to Dominic, thanking him for the time and the information.

* * *

Robert Wilkinson had spent a busy morning over at the forensic laboratory with Aoife, the assistant who had done the extra work on Tony Phelan's house at the request of Fiona Moore.

"We took the tiny samples that we recovered from the glass that had been smashed out of the back door. We magnified them, and found a few skin flakes still stuck to the glass, as well as a tiny patch of blood that had dried onto the outside. I got an accelerated DNA test carried out on the samples, and we compared them to the samples we had on file for when O'Neill was last in prison. Bingo! A match," she said.

"Nice one, Aoife. Can you say for sure that it was O'Neill that set the fire at Phelan's house?"

"No. That's up to you lot. But I can say he was there, and he came in contact with the glass in the back door after it was broken."

"Excellent. That should do it. Thanks very much. You're a star. Can you bang that in an email and send it across to me?"

"Sure. No problem."

Wilkinson went back to the station and rounded up four burly uniformed Gardaí. They set off in a marked Garda car for Sandymount where they were hoping to find Malachy O'Neill working on Glinn's building.

They arrived at the site, and Wilkinson went and spoke to the security guard he had met previously at the entrance.

"I'm looking for Malachy O'Neill. Can you tell me where I can find him, please?"

"Mal. Yeah, sure. He should be over in the store there. We just got a delivery." The security man pointed to a dark brown forty-foot container at the far side of the site, standing with its doors open. Wilkinson could see men inside.

He turned back to the squad car and signalled to the four Gardaí to join him.

"Right, lads. We're here to collect Malachy O'Neill. He's over there in the container."

The uniformed Gardaí needed no further encouragement and set off across the uneven ground to lift their quarry. They returned a few minutes later holding O'Neill by the arms.

"You can't just take me for no reason," O'Neill protested, "what am I supposed to have done?"

"Which is your vehicle, Mr O'Neill?"

"It's that blue van over there," O'Neill said, gesturing towards a very dirty and quite beaten-up old Ford parked at the roadside.

"May I have the keys please?" Wilkinson said.

"Don't you need a warrant or something?" O'Neill said somewhat nervously.

"Listen. Either you can give me the keys, or one of these men can jemmy it open with a wrecking bar. Now, which would you prefer?"

O'Neill said nothing, but rummaged in his pocket and fished out a set of keys, handing them to Wilkinson.

Wilkinson gave them to one of the Gardaí not holding O'Neill and the man went to the van, opening the rear door. A moment later, he shouted, "Here, Sarge," and held up a petrol can in a gloved hand.

"Good man. Bag it up and bring it along. We're going to have a chat with Mr O'Neill back at the station."

Chapter Thirty-Three

Jun's solicitor had left the station, and Jun returned to the cells. Burke went downstairs, and asked the sergeant to open up Jun's cell so that he could have a word.

"None of your heavy stuff now, Aidan," the wily old sergeant said. He had seen Burke rough up more than a few 'clients' in his time.

"Ah, there won't be a mark on him!" Burke quipped. "No, seriously, I only want a word with him. You can leave the door open and stand outside if you like?"

"Go on. You're all right."

Burke entered the cell and sat down beside Li Jun on the thin blue-vinyl-covered mattress that was the only furniture in the bleak, cold cell.

"Right, Li. I know you understand me, so here's what I'm going to tell you. We know you shot poor old Tony Phelan, but our evidence is very thin, just like your solicitor said. So, it's been decided upstairs that we'd be better sending you back to Shanghai. We're going to put you on board the China Skies freight plane tonight – we don't want a paperwork trail. Do you understand?"

"Yes, yes. Thank you, sir," Jun said, nodding his head vigorously.

"Wait. That's not all. In return for your freedom, I want your solemn undertaking that you won't come back here. If I find you here again, things will go very differently. Do you follow?" Burke said.

"Yes, yes. I will stay away. Promise."

"Right. Well, we'll collect you later and take you out to the airport. Meanwhile, get some rest. I'll arrange some food for you."

Burke stood up and left the cell.

"Thanks, Danny. See? He's untouched."

"Right, sir, and I never heard a word," the man said, tapping the side of his nose with his index finger.

* * *

When Burke got back upstairs, Moore told him that Wilkinson had brought in Malachy O'Neill. She also told him about the results from the forensic lab that placed O'Neill at the back of Tony Phelan's house at the time of the fire.

"Good. Nice one. OK. You'd better sit in with him – he's more used to dealing with fraud cases. But let him lead – he's been very helpful."

Moore went and found Wilkinson at his desk just finishing a sandwich.

"Hi, Rob. The boss has asked me to sit in on the interview with O'Neill. Are you OK with that?"

"Yeah, sure, I'd welcome it to be honest. I'm not very experienced with arsonists."

"Don't worry. We have him more or less banged to rights anyway. Did the lads find anything more in his van?" Moore said.

"Yes, they did. There were dozens of receipts scattered all around in the front of the van, and amongst them is a receipt for four litres of petrol on the night of the fire."

"Crikey – almost too good to be true. Eejit!"

"When you've finished your lunch, let's get on with it. I have another job coming up later. Has he a brief?" Moore said.

"Yes, he has. And not just a duty solicitor. Glinn has got some sharpshooter from one of those big places on the quays for him," Wilkinson said.

"Interesting. Actually, that might go against him in the end. Anyway, you lead, OK? And if you want me to take over, tap my foot under the table."

"Right. Let's do it!" Wilkinson drained his drink, crunched up the empty sandwich wrapper and threw it in the wastepaper bin.

* * *

The lawyer who had arrived to represent Malachy O'Neill was in his mid-thirties. He was immaculately presented in an expensive tailored suit, plain white shirt and silk tie. His black leather shoes were highly polished, and he spoke with an educated accent.

The solicitor was seated alongside his client with a yellow legal pad open in front of him and a black Mont Blanc pen. He was the first to speak when the detectives entered the room and took their seats.

"May I ask, Sergeant, why you have arrested my client at his place of work and dragged him here for questioning? What is he supposed to have done?"

"Your client is here to help us with our enquiries into a house fire in Marino where a man was found dead, Mr Corrigan. We believe your client may have set the fire."

"I didn't do nothing," O'Neill piped up.

"And I presume you have evidence to back up these very serious allegations?" Corrigan said.

Wilkinson ignored the question.

"Mr O'Neill, where were you on the night of October 17th last?" Wilkinson said.

"I dunno. Probably in the pub."

"And what pub would that be?"

"Jaysus, I don't know, do I? I don't keep a bleeding diary."

"So, to be clear, you can't actually say where you were on the night in question, is that right?" Wilkinson said.

O'Neill said nothing.

"Mr O'Neill, do you know the terrace of houses at the start of the Malahide Road in Marino?"

"No, I don't."

"Can you explain, then, how your DNA was found at the scene of a house fire at the end of that terrace where a man was found dead?"

"No comment," O'Neill said.

"Sergeant, can you tell me how this alleged DNA sample was collected?" Corrigan said.

"It was recovered from a piece of glass taken from the back door of the house, Mr Corrigan."

"And when was it collected, Sergeant?" Corrigan said.

"Recently," Wilkinson said.

"So, not on the night of the fire, then?"

"No, more recently than that."

"Well, really, Sergeant. Clearly that sample could easily have been contaminated, and if hasn't been gathered contemporaneously with the event, then I imagine it would not be admissible."

Wilkinson tapped Moore under the table with his foot.

"Look, Mr O'Neill, I'm not sure if you understand the seriousness of your position. A man died in that house. Whatever way you look at it, that's murder, and that's what we're looking at as of now," Moore said.

O'Neill looked pleadingly at Corrigan.

"Again, I ask, Sergeant, what actual evidence have you that my client was in any way involved with this unfortunate incident?"

"Mr O'Neill, how long have you worked for Mr Glinn?"

"Over five years now," O'Neill said.

"And isn't it true that, during that time, a number of properties belonging to Glinn have been damaged by fire?"

"No comment."

"You see, Mr O'Neill, I think Glinn is at it. Setting fire to listed properties so that he can redevelop them, and I think you're the man with the matches."

O'Neill shifted uneasily in his seat, and looked nervously at his solicitor.

"I wonder if I could have a few minutes to confer with my client, Sergeant?" Corrigan said.

"Fifteen minutes," Moore said and signalled Wilkinson to leave the room with her.

Outside, Moore said to Wilkinson, "Well done. I bet he coughs for the arsons if we let him off the murder."

"But he didn't actually kill Phelan, did he?"

"No, he didn't, and you'll note I was careful not to say that he did. But right now, he thinks he may have done, so we can use that as leverage. He's rightly spooked."

* * *

When Moore and Wilkinson went back in, Corrigan was the first to speak.

"Sergeant," he said, looking at Moore, "my client might be able to provide some information concerning the matters you raised earlier, but he is adamant that he had nothing to do with the unfortunate death of the homeowner in Marino."

"I see. Well, why doesn't Mr O'Neill give us what he's got, and we'll see what we can do?"

O'Neill spilled his heart out about Glinn's nefarious activities. He gave them details of three separate fires that he knew of, but stopped short of admitting that he had been responsible for burning the properties.

At the end of the session, Moore asked Wilkinson to charge O'Neill with arson and bail him. Corrigan placed the cap back on his Mont Blanc pen, and put it away in his expensive leather briefcase.

When they were back upstairs, Wilkinson asked Moore, "Should I go and get Glinn in?"

"No. Leave him for now. I'd like you to see if you can establish a link with McBrien first. Glinn won't be going anywhere – he has too much capital tied up in his developments."

Chapter Thirty-Four

It was a dry evening as Burke, Moore and Li Jun drove out to the airport to keep their meeting with Joe Donnelly. Moore was driving, and she noted that as she swung the car in through the gates of the Jet59 depot, there was no security guard present.

She stopped close to the exit from the pumping station, and had a good look round. There was no sign of Joe, so they stayed in the car. A few minutes later, a bowser came into the yard moving briskly. The vehicle was parked up, and Joe Donnelly emerged and walked over to Moore's door.

"All set then?" he said.

"Yes, we're good to go. I've explained to Mr Jun that as he isn't strictly speaking actually in the country, he can't leave on a normal scheduled flight without attracting all the wrong kind of attention. He seems happy to be going back in the freighter anyway," Moore said.

The three of them got out of the car.

"There's been a bit of a complication, I'm afraid," Donnelly said as they made their way to a portacabin where tea making facilities were set up for the night shift operators.

"Oh, what's that?" Burke said.

"I hear that they are going to do a customs inspection of the Shanghai flight this evening before it departs. That could be a problem for us. What if they find Mr Jun on board? He won't be on the manifest."

"Christ! Of all nights. How often does this happen?" Moore said.

"Every few weeks. I think they may have suspicions about those Presswell boxes. What are we going to do?" Donnelly said.

The group remained silent for what seemed like an age. Then Li Jun spoke up.

"Maybe I could hide on board. There is a special compartment at the back of the luggage hold. It's sometimes used for animals. I could go in there and wait till the flight is in the air, then the attendant could let me out."

"OK. That sounds like a plan. But is that compartment heated and air-conditioned? We wouldn't want you to freeze, Li," Moore said.

"Yes. They use it to carry animals, like dogs and cats. But it's good for humans too."

"OK. Let's do that then. As soon as the crew have left the plane, we'll put you on board, and you can go and hide in there. I presume the customs folks don't know about that place?" Burke said.

"Na. They're just concerned with matching the pallets to the manifest to make sure everything is properly declared. You know what they are like for paperwork. They even check our stocks every now and then to see that we're not making off with some Jet-A1. Did you know that you can use that stuff in your central heating at home?" Joe Donnelly said.

"No, I didn't know that. Has there ever been any issue with it?" Burke said.

"Now, do ye think we'd be daft enough to get caught at that kind of malarkey?" Donnelly said.

Burke looked at Moore and smiled. They both observed that Joe had said that they wouldn't be daft enough to actually get caught. He didn't say it didn't happen.

The small talk continued for a while longer till the noise of the China Skies freighter arriving on its stand interrupted them.

"Right. How are we going to do this, then?" Moore said.

"When the crew are off, I'll take Li here out with me in the fuel truck. I'll park on the side away from the cargo door and fuel her from there. No disrespect, Li, but I think Sergeant Moore should come out with us to see you safely stashed in your little hidey-hole."

"Yes, yes, OK," Jun said.

They watched as the giant cargo door lifted up into the night air, and counted the crew descending the steps onto the apron. There were five of them in all, as usual, and a small minibus whisked them away indoors for their meal.

Before they left the portacabin, Li Jun asked Burke if he could have his holdall back.

"Yes, Li. I have it here for you, but I've removed that vicious looking weapon you had in there. We wouldn't want any accidents, would we?"

Burke handed over the bag, and Li looked inside and grunted.

Donnelly and his mate Cathal sat in the front of the fuel truck with Moore and Li Jun in the rear seats of the twin cab as they drove out to the China Skies aircraft. When the fuel line was attached, Donnelly signalled to Moore, and she got out taking Li Jun with her. They ducked under the aircraft near the back where there was more headroom, and Li climbed into the cargo hold. He went to the animal compartment and opened the door.

"Make sure you tell the captain I'm in here. Tell him to send the flight attendant to get me when they have taken off. OK?"

"OK, Li. We'll be sure to let him know," Moore said.

With Li Jun secured, she clambered down again from the plane and re-joined Joe Donnelly who was sitting in the cab of his truck reading the Irish Daily Mirror.

"All good?" Donnelly said.

"Yep. Will you tell the captain about his extra passenger before he leaves?"

"Yes. I have to bring a docket up when the fuelling is finished and get him to sign it. I'll tell him then."

"Right. Well, I'm going to walk back to your depot. We're done here, and I'm sure Inspector Burke would like to get away. Thanks for your help."

"OK. See ya."

When the plane was fuelled with Jet-A1, Joe Donnelly went to the side of the truck and printed off the docket showing how many tonnes of fuel had been put on board. He tore off the sheet of paper, walked around to the steps of the plane and climbed up to the flight deck.

The crew hadn't returned from their meal break, so Joe left the docket on the pilot's seat, as he normally did, and then turned his attention to the panel of circuit breakers behind the co-pilot's position. He took the piece of paper that he had used earlier when he was talking to his mate the electrical engineer, and studied it.

The panel had nine rows of little buttons, and each row had fourteen circuit breakers along its length. Helpfully, they were clearly labelled. The one Joe wanted was in row D and was the tenth one across, according to his mate. The entire row was devoted to air-conditioning and heating, which looked about right to Joe.

He twisted the tenth button a half-turn anti-clockwise, and the little fuse like device popped out, with a tiny bright red tube protruding back into the innards of the panel. At the far end of the little red tube, there was a metal cap, which Dominic had told him was how the circuit was made. If a short occurred, the whole assembly popped out of its housing, breaking the connection and providing the flight crew with a visual clue as to which one was malfunctioning. Joe took a small piece of black insulating tape from inside the lapel of his jacket, and fixed it over the metal end cap of the circuit breaker. He then pushed it back into place, turned it half a turn clockwise, and stood up to see if there was any trace of his handiwork left behind. There was none.

As Joe Donnelly stood up, he said to himself, "This is for you, Tony. I hope the little bugger chokes nice and slowly – bastard!"

There was no customs inspection of China Skies flight seven-zero-five that night. It had been a ruse dreamt up by the fuellers to lure Li Jun into the secret compartment where he would meet his end.

The flight was loaded. The crew re-joined their aircraft, and the China Skies A300 took off from Dublin at 11:27 p.m. The crew were unaware of their additional passenger.

Chapter Thirty-Five

"Hi, Janet, it's Rob. How's it going?"

"Oh, hi Rob. All good. And you?"

"Fine thanks. Listen, I was wondering if you're free this evening after work?" Wilkinson said.

"Na, sorry, I'm washing my hair."

"Oh, OK. That's a shame."

Janet could hear the disappointment in his voice.

"Just kidding!" she said, giggling. "Yeah, I'm free. What have you in mind?"

"You know – a bit of grub and a few drinks. Nothing special."

"God, you really know how to woo a girl, don't you? But, yeah OK. But this time it's my treat, right?"

"If you insist. I'll call for you at, say, seven-thirty. OK?"

"Yeah, OK. See you then."

* * *

When Wilkinson arrived at Janet's apartment at just after seven-thirty, she invited him up. When he pushed open the door to number six, he was surprised to see that there was a table laid in the living room with a candle and a bottle of red wine, and two place settings. There was a lovely smell of cooking too.

Janet emerged from the kitchen area and walked over to Wilkinson, put her arms around him and gave him a long soft kiss.

"I thought we'd eat in. Is that OK?"

"Sure. Smells delicious, whatever it is. You didn't say you were a five-star cook!"

"That's exactly what it is," Janet said.

Wilkinson looked puzzled.

"Whatever – it's my speciality. Whatever with tossed salad and garlic bread."

Wilkinson kissed her again, and then she broke away saying, "Easy tiger. We don't want a burnt offering, do we?"

The meal tasted as good as it smelled. Janet had prepared a home-made lasagne which was cooked to perfection. It was accompanied by an unusual salad consisting of green leaves, olives, avocado, small tomatoes, scallions and baby oranges, and generously buttered hot garlic bread. The red wine she had chosen to accompany the meal was excellent too, and they consumed most of the bottle during the meal.

"Wow – that was amazing! Is there no end to your talents?"

"No, none. So, what have you been up to?" she asked as they sat on her comfy sofa having abandoned the table and decided to leave the clearing away till later.

Wilkinson told Janet about the arrest of O'Neill, and the fact that they had Glinn now well in their sights.

"But what we really need is some way of connecting Glinn to McBrien. O'Neill couldn't give us anything."

"Can I do anything to help?" Janet said.

"Hmm... maybe. Have you started looking for another job?"

"Yes, I have. In fact, I have an interview with one of the big companies in town the day after tomorrow. But they've said it's just a formality. They're very short-staffed. The market is really hotting up."

"If you told them about your culinary skills, it would seal the deal."

Janet punched Wilkinson's thigh.

"Cheeky," she said.

"There may be a way you could help. But I don't want you getting yourself into trouble. There's a lot of money at stake here, so it could get a bit nasty."

"Don't worry about me, I can look after myself."

"OK. Well, if you could get us copies of any emails that have been exchanged between Glinn and McBrien, that would be great. Don't stop to read them – just copy them onto a thumb drive. Everything you can find."

"OK. It'll give me an excuse to see you again anyway. But listen, I'm no policewoman, but wouldn't that be inadmissible or something if you obtained the emails without a warrant?"

"Ah, yes. But don't worry, I have a plan."

"I thought you might."

They kissed again.

* * *

The following morning, Wilkinson found Burke in his office.

"Come in, Rob, take a seat."

Wilkinson told the inspector about his meeting with Janet the previous evening, and what they had agreed.

"What's your plan?" Burke said, rather uneasily.

"Let's see what's in the emails. If there's anything incriminating in them, we can get a warrant to lift McBrien's computer, and of course he won't know that we've already seen them. We can put it down to enquiries relating to Glinn's activities."

"Sounds OK. Do you think Janet is in any danger?" Burke said.

"No, I don't think so. She's pretty smart. She'll be careful."

"OK. Well, make sure she is. Stay on it, Rob, will you? I don't like the idea of that guy O'Neill still being on the loose with his jerry-can."

"Right, boss."

* * *

Wilkinson sent a text to Janet as he was leaving the station at six-thirty in the evening. The traffic leading out of town was solid, and it took him nearly forty minutes to reach her apartment building in Ballsbridge.

As he pulled into the parking lot in front of the building, he looked at his phone, but there had been no response from Janet.

The main door to the apartment block wasn't properly closed, so Wilkinson went in and climbed the stairs to number six. What he saw when he got there alarmed him.

The door to Janet's apartment stood partly open, and the door jamb was ripped and splintered. There were large dents in the solid wooden door where it had clearly been bashed with something heavy in order to gain entry to the place. There was a light on inside.

Wilkinson pushed the door gently, at the same time calling out, "Janet, Janet, are you OK?" but there was no response.

He entered the flat. The place was a mess. Drawers had been pulled out, the table in the dining area was overturned, all sorts of stuff lay scattered around on the floor and on the furniture, and the kitchen cupboard doors were all open, as was the fridge.

Wilkinson called out again, and walked gingerly over to the bedroom, not knowing what he might find.

"Janet, are you there?" he called out again, but there was no response.

The bedroom was in the same chaotic state. All of Janet's clothes had been taken out of the wardrobe and the drawers and lay scattered around. The mattress on her double bed had been upended and sat at a crazy angle half on the bed and half on the floor. The bedside lamp lay smashed on the floor.

Wilkinson didn't touch anything and retreated back towards the front door. Then he called Fiona Moore.

"Hi, Fiona. Look, I'm out at Janet's place – you know the girl from the estate agents. It's been done over good and proper. And there's no sign of Janet, and I can't reach her on the phone. What should I do?"

"God, I'm sorry, Rob. You stay there. I'll come out immediately, and I'll bring a couple of officers from the robbery squad to go over the place. Any idea where she is?"

"No, none. I'm worried, Fiona. McBrien may have found out that she was copying files from the office PC and set the dogs on her."

"Yes, Aidan told me about that. Anyway, don't panic – not yet, anyway. While I'm driving out, do some door-to-door work on the nearby flats. See if anyone heard or saw anything. We won't be long."

Wilkinson went along the corridor to the next apartment and knocked on the door. He could hear a television or perhaps a radio which was turned up quite loud coming from inside the property, but there was no reply to his knocking.

He knocked harder, much harder.

Eventually, the door opened a few inches, and an old lady peered out. She was very elderly, with thinning grey hair set in tight curls, a creased and somewhat haggard face, and stood only about five feet tall.

Wilkinson introduced himself. He didn't want to alarm the woman, so he just asked her if she had heard any funny noises coming from outside her apartment in the last couple of hours.

It was clear that she was quite deaf, and after a difficult exchange, during which no invitation to enter the place was extended, Wilkinson concluded that the woman probably heard very little at all, ever. He thanked her for her time, and the door closed again. He could hear a chain being slid across inside.

Chapter Thirty-Six

Moore arrived quite soon, together with two plain clothes officers carrying some equipment to fingerprint the place.

"Hi, Rob, are you OK?" Moore said when she met Wilkinson standing outside number six leaning against the balustrade.

"No, not really. I can't contact Janet at all. I'm worried sick."

"Still nothing then. OK, let me get this lot set up and we'll go outside and have a chat. Try not to worry," she said touching him on his arm.

Outside, Moore and Wilkinson stood against her car.

"What will we do now? I'm afraid McBrien may have set that fucker O'Neill on her. She could be in real bother," Wilkinson said.

Just as he was allowing his imagination to paint some terrible mental images – he had become fond of Janet in the short time that they knew each other – his phone rang. He looked at the screen, "It's her!"

"Janet, Jesus, where are you? Are you OK?"

"Yes, of course, why?"

"Where are you?"

"I'm in Saint Vincent's. My mother was brought in earlier with breathing problems, so I came straight here from work. They made me turn my phone off. Why, what's up?"

"I'm at your place. Look, I'm afraid it's been broken into. The front door was smashed in, and it's in a fine old mess. We have a few Gardaí here looking for fingerprints. I'm sorry."

"It's hardly your fault. Anyway, Mum is a bit better now. They have her on oxygen, but they're going to keep her in overnight just to be safe. So, I'll come back. I'll be there is ten minutes. OK?"

"Yes, of course. See you then."

"See, I told you," Moore said with a smile. She could see the relief on Rob Wilkinson's face.

"Yeah, thank God she's OK. What now?"

"I want to stay here and talk to her. You can say hello, but then make yourself scarce. You shouldn't really be involved at all."

"Can I not stay?"

"No, Rob, you can't. If the break-in is in any way related to McBrien and Glinn, and it becomes known that Janet and you are an item, then our case is a blow-out. You must see that," Moore said.

"I suppose."

* * *

Janet arrived back a few minutes later. Wilkinson introduced her to Moore and they all went upstairs to her apartment. Janet was visibly shocked at what she saw before her.

"I'll give you a hand to straighten it up when the fingerprint guys are done. We'll have it sorted in no time, don't worry," Moore said.

"I have to get off, Janet. I'll call you later if you like. By the way, did you manage to get that copying of the files done?" Wilkinson said.

"Christ, Rob, give her a chance," Moore said.

"Yes, I did. I have the little memory thing in my bag. Hold on, I'll get it for you."

"Thanks. Sorry to bring it up. But I was concerned that it might have been here, and that's why you were broken into."

"Oh, I see. No, I didn't come home before I went to the hospital," she said, handing over a small black thumb drive.

"Thanks. Chat later," Wilkinson said, and left the apartment.

When he was gone, the two women started in Janet's bedroom, putting her clothes back into the wardrobe and straightening out the bed. In a few minutes, apart from the broken bedside lamp, they had the place more or less back to normal.

"I'm going to make some coffee. Would you like some?" Janet said.

"Yes, please. Thanks."

The two Gardaí that had been trying to collect fingerprints were packing up their kit in the living room.

"Anything?" Moore asked.

"Na, gloved up, I'm afraid. Nothing useful."

"Oh, I've just remembered," Janet said, "there's CCTV."

"Really? Where? I didn't see a camera anywhere."

"I know. It's concealed in the light fitting here," she said, pointing to an ordinary-looking glass fitting in the ceiling.

"The last occupant of this place was paranoid about security, and I never bothered to take it down. It records onto a little memory card and overwrites every day or two."

One of the burly Gardaí got a chair and climbed up to the light fitting.

"Yes, here we go. Neat."

When he descended, he had a small SD card in his hand.

"Do you mind if we keep this for now?" he said to Janet.

"'course not. That's fine. I'd forgotten all about it, to be honest."

"Great, thanks. I'll take it back to the station."

* * *

When there was just the two of them left in the apartment, and they had cleared up as best they could, they sat down at the dining table.

"Where are you going to stay tonight?" Moore asked.

"Gosh, I hadn't thought. I could get our maintenance guys out to fix the locks. They have a 24/7 emergency service for just this kind of thing. Then I could stay here."

"I'd prefer if you didn't. At least until we find out what's behind this. Why don't we book you into one of the hotels nearby for a couple of nights?"

"Do you think I'm in danger?"

"Maybe, maybe not. But Rob would never forgive me if anything happened to you. He's fond of you, you know."

"I know. It's mad, really. We've only just met, but he seems really nice. Have you known him long?"

"No. He's on secondment to us for this case. I hadn't met him before. What do you think of him?"

"He's lovely. It's funny. We seem so natural with each other. I haven't experienced this before. I hope it lasts – for a while anyway. Blimey, he's not married or anything, is he?"

"No, nothing like that. I doubt if he'd be seeing you if he was. He's not the type."

"How do you know he's not the type?"

"Janet, when you've come across all the different types of guys that I have in my working life, you get to know. Rob is one of the good guys. Trust me."

"I hope you're right. I'm in a bit deeper than I normally get with him, but for God's sake don't tell him."

"It'll be fine. Right, gather up your toothbrush and night dress, and let's go find you a hotel."

Chapter Thirty-Seven

Wilkinson slipped the little thumb drive into the USB port on his PC. Firstly, he virus-checked the device and found, thankfully, that it was clean. Then he applied a filter to the hundreds of emails, looking just for the ones between Glinn and McBrien, before sorting them into date order.

There were between sixty and seventy entries left when he had reduced them to the relevant ones, and he set about printing those off, starting with the latest and going backwards in time.

He then took the stack of paper to his desk and started reading. It didn't take him long to find what he was looking for. There were emails from McBrien with links to properties that were in poor repair and described as 'listed'. Several of them were of the Georgian kind, popular in parts of Dublin such as Mountjoy Square, Merrion Square, Fitzwilliam and so on. Other emails from Glinn talked about the price that these could be acquired for, and the development potential of the places in the future.

Wilkinson opened a new Excel spreadsheet and keyed in the headlines in date order along with the sender and recipient's name. When he had finished, he printed off the sheet and went looking for Inspector Burke.

* * *

While Wilkinson was busy with his analysis of the data that Janet had given them, Fiona Moore was getting to grips with the little SD memory card that they had removed from the camera in Janet's apartment.

She took it to a standalone PC that they had for just such a purpose. It wasn't connected to the network, in case whatever they might plug into it was virus-laden. She rooted in the drawer of the desk on which the PC rested, and found a multi-card reader. A few moments later, she had fired up the VLC programme and the video began to roll. It was surprisingly high definition for such a humble device. The first sequence which was dated the day before the robbery showed Janet and Rob Wilkinson on the sofa getting rather cosy. She quickly fast-forwarded past that bit, feeling a tad embarrassed. In the next clip, Moore could see the dark shape of a young man coming into view. The camera was clearly one of those that was activated when motion was detected, so as not to waste the modest amount of storage afforded by the little card.

As she watched, she could see the burglar rummaging around.

"What filth are you watching," Dónal Lawler quipped as he came over to where Moore was engrossed, and looked over her shoulder.

"Filth indeed. We took this from a concealed camera in Janet's apartment. Good, isn't it?"

Just then, the face of the intruder came into clear view as he searched the top of a cupboard looking for saleable items.

"Well, I never," Lawler said, "that's only Shifty McClure, isn't it? Stop it next time his ugly mug comes into view."

Moore did just that.

"You know this guy then, Dónal?"

"I sure do. I thought he was locked up, but obviously not. Yes, he broke into a shop on Shelbourne Road a couple of years back. He climbed up on a roof, and got in through a very high window that wasn't alarmed because it was so inaccessible. But when he entered the shop, he fell down onto the floor and twisted his ankle very badly. The owner found him the following morning, asleep in a drunken stupor surrounded by an empty vodka bottle and several empty crisp packets, his ankle swollen to the size of a turnip. The judge was fed up of seeing him in his court again, so he gave him two years. Not the sharpest knife in the drawer, our Shifty."

"Could there be any connection between this character and McBrien and Glinn?"

"No, not a chance. Shifty is just a small-time opportunist burglar. He's no property mogul. I'll get uniform to pay a house call and get him in. When we show him this, he'll cough for it, and then at least he'll be off the streets for another year or two."

"Well, that's a relief, anyway. At least Janet can go back to her place as soon as the door is fixed up."

* * *

"Nice one, Rob. But, of course, you do realise that we can't use any of this as evidence given the way it was obtained," Burke said.

"Yes, I know, sir. But now we can get a warrant and go in and seize McBrien's PC to make it legit."

"And what would be the basis of such a warrant?"

"'Information received' should do it. Do you want me to ask the Super?" Wilkinson said.

"Yes, and I've been thinking. This business with Glinn and McBrien is more in the line of fraud than murder. And O'Neill didn't actually kill poor old Tony Phelan after all. Would you be happy to take the whole lot back to the fraud squad, and continue the case from there? Not that I want rid of you – you've been a great help on this case. But we need to concentrate on tying up the loose ends around the fire and the death, so we'll be busy enough with that."

"Yes, OK, sir. That sounds like a sensible move. I'll get all the stuff together and ship out later. I'd like to do the call on McBrien's place as early as possible, though. He may already smell a rat, and we don't want him destroying any evidence."

"Yes, I agree. OK. I'll get the Super to issue a warrant and you can get on with it. I'll have it in an hour or so."

"Thanks, sir."

When Wilkinson got back to his desk, he called Janet on his mobile.

"Hi. It's me. You OK?"

"Yeah, great thanks. That hotel bed was a lot more comfortable than mine at home, even if it was half empty," Janet said.

"Listen, will McBrien be there at all today?"

"Yes. He has an appointment with a client here at one o'clock. A couple are buying and selling and I think they are going to give both transactions to us. Why?"

"Excellent. Well, could I ask you to make yourself scarce at that time? Take a nice long lunch at around 12:45 and stay out of sight till later."

"Hmm... OK. What's this about?"

"I can't say, love, just trust me. And are you getting your apartment door fixed up?"

"Yes. There're workmen there now doing it. I'll probably move back in later. Fancy coming around?"

"I'll call you later. Oh, wait, is it today that you have your interview?" Wilkinson said.

"They called and deferred it till tomorrow. But they've offered me the job anyway, just subject to confirmation after they see me in the flesh."

"Cool. Is the money OK?"

"Yes, it is. A nice increase on what I'm getting here, that's for sure. But listen, Rob, what's actually going on with McBrien? Had he anything to do with the break-in at my place?"

Wilkinson reassured Janet that there was no connection to the burglary, and told her the story of Shifty McClure.

"Thank God for that. But to be honest, I'll probably move out anyway when I get the new job. You know how it feels when your home has been broken into like that."

"Yes, I do. I have to go now, love. I'll call you later on. And remember what I said about lunchtime."

"OK. Talk later. Bye."

Chapter Thirty-Eight

It was late in the afternoon when Burke, Moore, Wilkinson and Lawler got together to go over the day's activities.

"Let's start with you, Dónal. What have you got?"

"Shifty. We lifted him just before lunchtime. These fellas don't get up too early. There he was all snuggled up in his duvet, Janet's iPad on the floor beside his bed. At first, he tried to deny everything, but when we showed him the video footage, he confessed pretty quickly after that. He said it was his mam's birthday in a few days, and he didn't have any money to buy her a pressie. I suggested he didn't use that in his defence!"

"Where is he now?"

"They've taken him back to the Joy. He was only out on licence anyway, so he'll be there for a good while after this."

"Excellent. One less tea leaf we have to worry about. Well done all," Burke said.

Wilkinson was the next to speak.

"We raided McBrien's offices at one o'clock. The man himself was there. He was pretty angry. He had a couple of clients that he was trying to do business with. We took his PCs and I've had a quick look at them. All the emails that

Janet gave us are still there, so that should put him right in the frame for lots of suspicious transactions. Like you said, boss, I've spoken to my lot over in Harcourt Street and they are more than happy to run with it."

"Right. Nice work. What about Glinn and O'Neill?"

"I suggest we bring Glinn in for questioning. Now that we have the emails from McBrien legitimately, we can probably nail him. But should we leave that to the fraud squad, boss?"

"Yes, I think so. But we have O'Neill for arson in any case to keep the figures up."

"Are you going to try and put the murder of Phelan on him as well, boss?" Moore asked.

"No. No point. Any half-witted brief would tear it to shreds. I'm afraid we'll just have to write that one off to experience."

"I wonder if Li Jun is safely back in Shanghai by now?" Lawler said.

"Somehow, I think maybe not," Burke said.

"Oh? Is there something I should know?"

"Let's just say, the team out at Jet59 may have had their own way of seeking revenge for Tony's death. But we're not going there, are we?" Burke said.

"No, sir," the three others said in unison.

"Right, well, Heffernan wants to see me, so I'd better go on up. Not a bad day's work for us, given the circumstances. See you all in the morning."

When they got back outside, Moore went over to Rob Wilkinson.

"Hi Rob. How do you like being in the movies?"

"What? How do you mean?"

"That camera footage we took from Janet's apartment. It didn't just record Shifty, you know," she said with a broad grin.

"Christ! Are you serious? What have you done with it?" Wilkinson said, his cheeks colouring.

"Now, that's for me to know and you to find out, Sergeant. Maybe I'm keeping it for the Christmas party!" She walked off, smirking.

* * *

Burke sat uneasily at the opposite side of Superintendent Jerome Heffernan's desk. The senior man was reading some loose papers he had on his desk, not looking up. This was not a good omen.

Heffernan looked up, at last.

"Have you anything to tell me, Aidan?"

"Eh... about what, sir?"

"Oh, you know, this and that. Like the China Skies flight to Shanghai last night."

"I don't know what you mean, sir."

"Don't fuck with me, Aidan. I've had a call from the Chief of the Airport Police. Apparently, that flight had to go into Stansted to pick up some additional cargo, and here's the interesting thing, a couple of greyhounds destined for some big race in China. You'll never guess what they found when they opened up the animal hold on the plane."

"Oops!" Burke said.

"Oops indeed. Lucky for you he was still alive – just."

"We didn't have anything to do with that, sir. We just delivered him to the plane. Whatever happened after that was nothing to do with the Gardaí. Where is he now?"

"Funnily enough, we don't know. He was in the little sick bay in the airport recovering. A couple of hours later, an air ambulance arrived from Geneva along with some diplomatic heavies from China. Stansted were persuaded to give him up, and he flew out later on – destination unknown."

"Well, that's the end of that then, isn't it, sir?"

"Maybe. But if you say you had no part in this, then someone out at the airport must have been involved," Heffernan said.

"Yes, but there's no way we could bring any charges. Where's the evidence, for starters?"

"You're right, much as I hate to admit it. You've sailed very close to the wind on this one, Aidan. Just think of what could have happened if the Chinaman ended up dead on our patch. Or if the plane had come down as a result of some interference by the lads out at the airport."

"If, if. If me aunt had balls she'd be me uncle, with respect, sir."

"True. But for God's sake, man, be careful, will you? I'm getting too near my pension to end up directing traffic on Tory Island."

Heffernan opened the drawer of his desk and took out a pair of Waterford Crystal cut glasses and a bottle of very special Irish whiskey. He poured two generous measures of the deep amber liquid and handed one to Burke.

Heffernan held up his glass in a sort of toast.

"Sometimes, you just have to do what you have to do. Sláinte!"

Epilogue

Wilkinson moved back to the Fraud Squad, taking the case of McBrien and Glinn with him. It was a difficult one, and it took the Gardaí almost a year of investigation before they were in a position to bring charges. The matter did eventually come to court, and Glinn was fined heavily for his involvement – a fine which he easily paid from the proceeds of the development in Sandymount. McBrien didn't fare so well. Word got out in the trade that he was crooked, and his business faded to nothing. He eventually closed up shop, and when last heard of, he was driving a white van delivering parcels for one of the courier companies.

Janet got her new job with the big firm in Dublin. They put her on sales, and she was highly successful. She soon earned enough commission to buy her own apartment in Dundrum, and had a camera installed, similar to the one that was so useful when she was burgled, along with other security measures.

Rob Wilkinson and Janet continued to see each other and developed a solid relationship that persists to this day.

O'Neill was brought to court on several charges of arson. He had done a deal of sorts with the Gardaí in exchange for information that helped their case against Glinn, so his punishment was light. He got a suspended sentence and continued to work in the building trade.

Li Jun was never heard of again after he departed Stansted in the air ambulance. Flightradar showed that the little jet had set off in an easterly direction and stopped briefly in Turkey on its way to China. Whether Jun had been offloaded during the stop-over was never revealed.

Joe Donnelly and his crew continue to fuel planes of all shapes and sizes out at Dublin Airport to this day. A few months after the events surrounding the death of Tony Phelan, China Skies ceased its flights in and out of Dublin, and the route was taken over by Cargolux.

The Americans infiltrated Presswell Exacta as they had said that they would. Alterations were made to the microchips going to China, but they were discovered by the Chinese importers and, later that year, the Chinese terminated their contracts with the company. The new contracts that Guy Anderson had promised never materialized, and with virtually no business Presswell closed down, going into liquidation. Flanagan had kept a sizeable amount of cash back from the company, and within a year had started a new business manufacturing drones. The Americans are keeping a close eye on that operation.

Billy Phelan took Burke's advice. He appointed Donohoe Turner and Montague in Dublin to look after his interests in Tony's house. It took a long time, but matters were eventually settled, and the burnt-out shell of the house was demolished. It had been sold to a developer who went on to get planning permission for five blocks of apartments on the school's land, and Billy received almost half a million dollars from the proceeds. Elsie O'Brien, who had followed the matter as closely as she could, was disgusted.

There was no fallout from the various irregularities that this case had generated as far as Jerome Heffernan was concerned. He remained a little uneasy for some months, half-expecting some repercussions from the Department of Foreign Affairs, but none came.

He resolved to keep a very close eye on Burke in future.

Character List

DI Aidan Burke – a senior Garda officer attached to Store Street Garda Station, wrestling with some personal issues

DS Fiona Moore – Burke's number two whose sole purpose in life seems to be to make her boss look good

Detective Dónal Lawler – a shrewd junior detective

Sergeant Walsh – the desk sergeant from Dalkey Garda Station

Jim O'Donnell – a senior firefighter with the Dublin Fire Brigade

Elsie O'Brien – lives in the house next door to Tony Phelan

Tony Phelan – an airport worker with American connections

Billy Phelan – Tony's brother who lives in New York

Malcolm O'Higgins – the state pathologist

Simon – O'Higgins' assistant

Mr Davern – the manager at the Jet59 aircraft fuel company

David – receptionist at Jet59

Cahir Flannery – not the name of the Presswell Exacta director

Majella – the receptionist at Walker Hodge

Gerald Walker – a somewhat devious accountant

Pascal Fleming – an Inspector in the Garda Fraud Squad

Danny – the desk sergeant in Store Street

Trevor – Moore's bank manager

Maureen – Superintendent Heffernan's PA

Jerome Heffernan – head of the Detective Unit in Store Street

Guy Anderson – a visitor from the US

Joe Donnelly – works at Jet59 fuelling aircraft

Cathal – Joe's helper

Frank McBrien – an estate agent

Paul Glinn – a builder

Mick Tyrrell – a dog handler

Cesar – a German shepherd dog

Denis Kelly – the storeman at Presswell Exacta

Cian Flanagan – the real name of the Presswell Exacta director

Li Jun – an unwelcome visitor from Shanghai

Andrew Green – a solicitor

Malachy O'Neill – a builder

Jimmy Mulvihill – a Garda

Phil and Aoife – forensic officers

Janet Fallon – a pretty blonde who works with McBrien

Marie Keogh – Chief Operating Officer of Dublin Airport Authority

Dominic – an aircraft electrician

Mr Corrigan – a solicitor

Shifty McClure – a small time thief

If you enjoyed this book, please let others know by leaving a quick review on Amazon. Also, if you spot anything untoward in the paperback, get in touch. We strive for the best quality and appreciate reader feedback.

editor@thebookfolks.com

www.thebookfolks.com

ALSO IN THIS SERIES

A man killed in a desolate alley. A woman attacked in her home. And two detectives who must connect these events, and hunt down a killer who doesn't give a damn.

The first murder mystery in this Irish crime fiction series by bestselling author David Pearson.

A man is found dead in his car in a forest outside of Dublin. Very dead. There is quite a mess. The police suspect foul play and call in the detectives. It is not long before another body is found in the area. A full-scale murder inquiry is launched. Can DI Aidan Burke and DS Fiona Moore collar the killer?

OTHER BOOKS BY DAVID PEARSON

In the Galway Homicides series:

Murder on the Old Bog Road (Book 1)
Murder at the Old Cottage (Book 2)
Murder on the West Coast (Book 3)
Murder at the Pony Show (Book 4)
Murder on Pay Day (Book 5)
Murder in the Air (Book 6)
Murder at the Holiday Home (Book 7)
Murder on the Peninsula (Book 8)
Murder at the Races (Book 9)

Available in paperback and free with Kindle Unlimited

A woman is found in a ditch, murdered. As the list of suspects grows, an Irish town's dirty secrets are exposed. Detective Inspector Mick Hays and DS Maureen Lyons are called in to investigate. But getting the locals to even speak to the police will take some doing. Will they find the killer in their midst?

When a nurse finds a reclusive old man dead in his armchair in his cottage, the local Garda surmise he was the victim of a burglary gone wrong. However, having suffered a violent death and there being no apparent robbery, Irish detectives are not so sure. It will take all their wits and training to track down the killer.

When the Irish police arrive at a road accident, they find evidence of a kidnapping and a murder. Detective Maureen Lyons is in charge of the case but, struggling with self-doubt, when a suspect slips through her fingers she must act fast to save her reputation and crack the case.

A man is found dead during the annual Connemara Pony Show. Panic spreads through the event when it is discovered he was murdered. Detective Maureen Lyons leads the investigation but the powers that be threaten to stonewall the inquiry.

Following a tip-off, Irish police lie in wait for a robbery. But the criminals cleverly evade their grasp. Meanwhile, a body is found beneath a cliff. DCI Mick Hays' chances of promotion will be blown unless he sorts out the mess.

After a wealthy businessman's plane crashes into bogland it is discovered the engine was tampered with. But who out of the three occupants was the intended target? DI Maureen Lyons leads the investigation, which points to shady dealings and an even darker crime.

A local businessman is questioned when a young woman is found dead in his property. His caginess makes him a prime suspect in what is now a murder inquiry. But with no clear motive and no evidence, detectives will have a hard task proving their case. They'll have to follow the money, even if it leads them into danger.

When a body is found on a remote Irish beach, detectives suspect foul play. Their investigation leads them to believe the death is connected to corruption in local government. But rather than have to hunt down the killer, he approaches them. With one idea in mind: revenge.

One of the highlights of Ireland's horseracing calendar is marred when a successful bookmaker is robbed and killed in the restrooms. DI Maureen Lyons investigates but is not banking on a troublemaker emerging from within the police ranks. Her team will have to deal with the shenanigans and catch a killer.

Manufactured by Amazon.ca
Bolton, ON